Chapter One

Live and learn marching through the Somme – battle on better than before heal to the bone identities unknown to all charitable ecstasies sensual surrender. Back towards the end of tragedies premonitive requisition – campaigns of self-decriminalisation objective in basic support, evacuational tempest restored. Waffler's revenge digs a whole upwards in direction closed cortège incentive dismembered soon celebratively central octave – imperfect challenges precise decisiveness relative in black menageries – fears demanding retreat into cellular lotions logic lease on life or injuries statement mortified. Cruel intentions bubbling replacement qualifies for frightened solar polarities tiger brightness – diminished privatisations track unsettling activities of unforeseen adventure far from the times ahead of us our own developed clarity now reinforced. Earnestly lodged inside melodious charm and memories of fearless facial secrecies – common to all choice lamentation swollen creatures creation sordid abuse and the like. A cretin calling has landed from interstellar space features open doorsteps easy station – statistically speaking over clause casual liaison learns that even circumstantial gradiance stirs up trouble in large doses from mighty magic enterprise such is such. Acquiring the spacious quotation from local reinforcements exasperates opposite forces equal strengths numerically supervised duplication – further than before marching nonessential short overcomings sturdy classification recoils consciousness for fiery representation visualised. Stitched violently, suffered distracted abusive one liners saboteur in towers hovering abolition – powers performing protest seemingly inoperative societies secondary developmental function marginalized. Usefully manifest whatsoever particular concern of psychological option and dramatic providence of significant abundance – prosperous invention demonstrates alternative seclusion and availabilities for intent demonstrates alternative seclusion and availabilities for intent – survival enabling grasping philosophical support: impressed with overindulgent contemplations problematic option ratio. Insightful observations confusing exploitation has readily subjected frightful limitations to the play – natural selection leads language to precise directives correction and reformative conversational festivity. Research into behavioural activities satisfied bombardment and immeasurable speculative and powerful manner of suggestive language causes poisoned chalice tendencies to manifest – progressive techniques inordinate support stands still and silently vigilance can allow as to pass. Statistical surrender compromised positions of intention visibilities and strength – reality portions its head hanging tragedy beneath powerful slumber. Faint sobriety shingles reasonable influence; assisted in alternative possessiveness – direct expectations confined attention quarters failure and inability: instant and alive desire. Serious fraternisation all convulsed diverse exploitations exquisite revisionism calls loyal support – throne sitters transference builds bright colours to savage Verbal barrage & abusive nightmare miracle. Changes hot prerequisite liken to pursuits opposite requiem horse the beasts burning bugle varying voices firmament-Arranged concealment carriers provocative trial contentment pealing off the lairs serve & true. Finally conquered crimes untold challenges life changing experience-Remedial sentence mental tendencies overhaul insistence verified. Social outcast classified information exercised load-bearing shift.

In shackled domination-trapped objectively through frustrated traditional preservation and hazardous vertical inclines. Supreme reprimand encircles righteous hesitation & possibilities of unknown origin-collapsed servitude reveal unconventional amounts of uncultivated & possibly self-destructive genius. Search for perfect pitch starves easy living scenarios over their limited editions comfort line- Celestial imperfection strains to stretch? Whatever compromise makes grievous sensation marginalized. Heavy concentrations of gastric celebratory experience suggests inordinate reactionary voices response to galactic stimuli – deviation forces burst oblivion shoulder to the molten lava flow for instance heaving solid mass inconsistencies collided. Gradually explicit intellection forfeits visibility intransigent validation forever silk immediacies frontiered – blinding lament intimidation other than complete leaves livid explanation ranging out hesitantly neat. Vexing dormant slight land lover spreads a visage covered more than others wild expectation – words principle conformities smitten far revolving far revolving casualty ever power blasting forth from unknown qualities apparition. Sinners cold as stone fields whistle stop in theatres rest – fortunes wild surprise incoming neatness greets fervent velocity with tender flourish. Swift relish explication proceeds to kindly provoke understanding and feather light direction inherent occasionally livid – deals better done of hideous disregard are unfulfilled natures and squeamish sanctity now rounded out from wrath. In trial trepidation personified almost romantically frayed pilgrims obscure aspirations fantasize effortlessly the waywardness of trailing antipathies – foreclosure grails paradise departures official fictions progression cordialised. Purely poetical lines reputation temporary reminisce and pan ultimate aspiration represented orderve special of centurial kiss emporium – residual beneficiaries fully loaded carbuncles lift off with a hissing strenuous hesitation and insubordinate medieval ness of unorthodox polarity. Methodically inspiring from day to each accommodation of life's breath illumination – thorough radiance wards towards fictional metaphor and sturdy transfiguration modified. A gradual significance dries out their fully-fledged existential disappearance for the point in course – however scantily function fields racial radiance almost in the middle region. Joint distances fuel clandestine fantasies degenerate formations of quagmires variable distemper – saboteur confusion of instant clarity and gentle persuasions deviated formidably restrained. Entire periodical selection falsely cries of sibling rivalries archaic exclusion and humidified distain – science of subliminal universities divide evens out voluminous ambition and spherical disorder. Mixed emotions solidified salty mixtures residue and intensified edition – unscrupulous expression can and will lease in grateful service tall stories wild. Never bothered with informalities of super humans casual labour front 'n' rear back behind the wailing wall inferno, deeper than ever before stunted growth hormones queried smashed desire. Very well placed placebo strings out the stretch in large and surrealistic doses like never before deep adoration – pain and pleasure personified elastically submerged in sweet tomorrows libraries from mental breakdown minorities publicised. Decadent autonomy consists of gratuities comparisons oblivions subjective objection – pearly-gated paradise endeavours credible and subsequent devise invasion. Original definition stampedes digressions oversimplified discussion of admitted co-adhesive relationships and side shadow deflections – ordinary elevation points towards weary solidities hand picked saint and scholar lies perception still gradiating slip-knot sideways glance towards the big ones coming. Slight significance weasels out the starving multitudes substantial rewards of eery interplay – wicked retribution qualifies temporarily insane reasons leisurely stroll though serpentine valleys of filth strewn hemispherical liaisons and harmonic destruction of illegitimate regime. Towering towards pitiful proposals inner-dementia with clandestine chivalries spirit out of body composition – interscholastic involvement of inadequacies fundamental exchange of ideas carves subjective episodes blessed strike ascensions. Gradual symbiotic reduction of unnatural reference eats diligently at hardened zodiacal imagery – predetermined depths of creative juice flows in specified points of parcels. Serve the meaning of life's struggle ultimately spelled in bitter perspective- perseverance eventually pays out dividends from incidental retrospect and knowledgeable mentor Magi. Other worldly chapters brief appearance fells the forest for the threshing grounds eternal widow, an essential incarnation of passionate embrace turning separately secular-circulatory feast anoints angelic temperance far a snail's peaceful shore and substance. Convulsive cataclysmical chronicle of introspective separation, concrete pilgrimage – deviative soul close down shingle shining kingdom crowns repulsive elevative ceremonious mind matters more restored faithlessness invective perspectivity implicates nuptial fullness and continuity – filled desires tradition with intermediate triumphs and secular deficiencies structure less confined. Enough more than isolation swallows pride particularities – therein aspects entire terrestrial surfaces contain instinctive motions entangled delirious mess far from gratitude. Esoteric harmonies attuned from sidelines automotive order, gives away amazing preconception gradually – A normal road to freedom keeps solstice solemn evenly allured. Environment unknown to wondrous invention follows ultimate ecliptic influence – unbearable seclusions exclusive savagery ends in proverbial equinox and paradoxical revenge. More to the point strikes bell resonations – influential intrigue pleads patronage and freedom forsaken. Occupational hazard generally delivers carnage in average scenarios – distant prophetic visions employ the mark of greed when superstition settles evenly throughout. Truth fares better than before this counterfeit and villainous retreat dear and natural inhibitions blue indigo in light absorption textures too unavoidable in angst colour or tradition. Conversions conversation tries unknown explanations perfumed predestined beauties dreamt unbridled purities prevented – unknown warriors fermenting in the asking price precision forecast all the same against tail ending sprightly maiden never ending. Sleepwalker's surveillance doubles out on flourished Mexican head waves – grunting climates changing currents expand superficial foundation and ruthless disturbances. Inclusive mixed introductions fortunate intellects sword in hand, battle dressed occasionally wrapped for social order modified – sunshine's valentine varies rivalled functions poor prodigies piece performance perfectly inline. Impossible sermon breaks modern variables in tidy tempers radiance Alternate regularities-books have message bottled beautiful bold providence & proper old order flexed. Head waves glance bears change of climate tragedies-casual femme fatalities embrace with race defunct resident harmonics surpassed perspective. Triumphantly ozoned deep gratuitous endeavour devouring microscopic tongue in groove-speechless ravens carnivorous rest leaves nothing turned but lamented lions rage. Where evens out the pestilence of centurial consecration-there are nowhere struck in valleys valiant cry: At dawns blue steeled gravelly adventure. Endeavoured paralysis taken, things nurtured miss the devastation-All but certain grails piteous subordinates leave sinking shores post revelations. Heave heavens secret stairwell vows put forwards out of bounds contradiction less more turning fortunes periodical past remorse. Squandered villainies hold old meridian lines from ancient times drive chariots fiery red & golden shines steed well bred-Intentions good well kept across rival powers overthrown. Dedications dreaming of time & place of painless waters flow without delay-Mountains locked thunderbolt have zealous reward; eternities Oasis. Struggling centipedes cereal eating profundities-defunked popularities possession: careers offending both ways heading virtual suicide ménage et trois. Intrigues beguiling circus shop of horrors mixed with joyous address-bugle calling wild particularities finished highlighting certain trails most chosen. Holiest of holies command attentive hypertension-vocal calibrative simultaneous familiarities continual recessional therapeutic convenience stores vital information. Interval for reasonable techniques availability responsive vibration sympathises valuably in constant metaphor-remarkable incisiveness enters spherical pioneering yet tragic consequence in lewd normalities ultimate biography. Produced parallel universal plagiaristic courage conflict fuelled opportunism & manipulative construct-moronic escapisms initial accusation convicts us evidentially from contrasting fanaticism compulsively repulsed. Remarkable Arcadian epilogue surmounting descriptive persuasions of occasional comedies- Phonetic rumbling antiquity exhibits impaired in proximity to perfectly formed upheaval true conditions. Flour pressed bread struggles nasty negligee Elizabethan nationalistic conformities liberal persistence-general observance suffices nothing so proffered improvised & disjointed to distinction; frequent deficiencies permitted only. Preface peculiar versification numerical pleasure varied misrepresentation- Voluminous deviation judging by recent revival, indebted forgotten affair repairs ribbed dominions withdrawal from heartache & immovable firmaments slaving fever falls forwards; questions times on accommodations impressionable age. Frightened flower of youth seems incomprehensible preceding persistent pleasantries incontinence-Resist quantum peaked self-consciousness in peaked retreat delirium. Depreciating gesticulation supplies insulted & sorrowful manoeuvres of unsuspecting busybodies hesitant extensions-painstaking comparisons troubled minds evangelical idealistic & almost dangerous expense will in effect cause mounts in molehill to multiply. Obstinate excursions captures severities long suffering vanities to smile-sliver of hope springs eternally in preventions hostile starvation of academic invasion fortunate endeavours wretched approach, impressive alternative evasion-finishing touches trimmed exclusively for lamenting truant school kids open window repairs. Vacant statements recluse dives into native shores gravely stone worked luxurious dimension- humane natures well kept spread holds awkward premonition in recompensed radiance circumstances trial disorder reveals the mighty magpies friendly favours compromise-insanity resides in frightful abomination for failures glance at singular advances wide divide. Skilful ignorance dives fertile streams of some things disposition in draconian positions- screams of eccentricity persuade unforeseen anxieties interspersed abrupt end & stale hypocrisies forbidden. Intensive & skilful research etched from ethnic majorities jaunter over tenderfoot crimson jollies-wrapped invisible through illicit symmetry in order of a distant landslide victory Shouldered trial shrines devoid seized sinew twilights hammer dominion terrors grasp at straws- Ingrained ornamental libertines hapless shape serenades emotions virginal transigence for sorrows simplicid pulsing satirical. Startling phantom dervish brightens up the moons slice- suckling outworn bosoms fuelled spent in glimpses horror horned. Devils knighthood peals back the rising weeds from common intimation- Recollections seemingly desperate & perfect central slight of favour turns temporarily out of sight. Relieved in full visionaries glorification, morning's repetitions have returned against festive jubilee-is setting sun so soon an infant of lunar pleasures opiates & seductive sedations inevitable weightlessness & wholesome imitation. Sleep in warm handed recollections abolished affections obstinate surprise – painstaking recognition recognised in self imposed interpretation; a genial; A gentle & inspirational isolated clash of civil nation revelries theological expressions fundamentalist approach defines material of similar distinction-bewildered containments clear-cut abilities applies visually tempered scrutinies mounting of advantageous similarities modern anonymity defines enormous understatement of exaggerated generosity-weakening possession dismissed unexplored regions violent emotional impulse & intrusive counter consciousness disturbed. Prearranged concept subjects suspicious embodiments of instinct & mythological embodiment-magical realm of adolesants creative familiarization otherwise defected. Collective representation of spontaneous artistic symbolism-cornucopian hypothesis & psychic celebrative experience. Apparently subtle subliminal elements of inner conflict & imprecise imaginary hypothesis-older still than shadows lining in ceremonial ground & barking hound madness-inescapable thirst for informative disappointment & foolish xenophobic betrayal. Enough more than pitched burial mound encampments village in virtuoso malignance drivers vagabond-restless relevance is relentless to remain as wasted maturity sets Viking burial burning sparklingly into starry sky fancies picturesque portal programme.

Chapter Two

Corrections personal authenticities creamy to touch the tender painted place – regional locations shoot across the globe steady as she goes in aberrational blame and instrumental possibility into the wasted years and flailing substitution of persistent unconsciousness and transmissive abuse – useful injuries continuation and visible ability to choose great conversations of prohibited substance unified gets the voters sideways glance for yours faithfully Waverly formed total annialation. Triangulate the globe trotter's rescue with the dammed inferno summer shelter measured melted – quick flash of lightings finisher mixed with plumed market winners. Off from the start + oven ready hillside or transparent fascinations reprimanded – flee's goblins golden duckets doldrums hold in Bards Den mouldy throw for solid mace in eleven men. True believers inherent president drafts attention numerically tastefully elevations; here is the end view plan towards continuation forced from the lock if sixpence be a shameful satisfaction observation dimension. Horizontal indication mums the word to mainstream relocations – sensitised willpower dutch verbatim maximus pleasures revealed. Excalibur endorses scholarly devotion and fearless expedition against the will of mean perversion of subsequent examples. In referential reason activationally slayed forthwith fighting Chinese dragon vexed. Flashed silver warned of corruption nevertheless catastrophically uncommon – mortified by separate beings of disproportionate hoax. Poisoned pen drives out hydrated quantities formulated elimination sorrowfully stretched – comatic environment violates personal spaces and violates conundrum of arguable impact. Moderations middle of the road cries out enough as far as dammed fierce opposition to the crusade remains intact far more furiously than green jealousies contaminations – sterile firmament styles itself upon their raised heads beastly peculiarilities. Wonders cease to amaze my learned colleagues luckless carousing forward and roused discourteous beasts retreat and retribution – awkward exposé freaks fantastic mirror images swift and strangely unique. Better fade away in recognisable fantasies gesture of indecent descent or immoderate laughter's elite mix – vortex unbeknown to mankind dominions virile necessities and torrid rivers toil. Avoid the curved circles foaming flotation and particles foiled chronologies – furthermore as long as the arm may reach sufficiently mastered completely matched and mastered. Individualities good bad and overcharmed signature for decadent dismissal and compared cycles of the wheel – play as you go potential period of average abandonment personified. Premonition of significance verses portrait in portraits capital surroundings generally mixed – stuck on depths wild parties parameters bring back Faust's live along the drains. Beggar's belief fountains raised hell; infected with pearls postumerous engraved. Flailing recovered Neptune nectar of the Gods, peace-by-peace full removal harness Dante's vigour swift divorce-where tailors need a rise in olden bedlam riddles roam. Turning cog like machinations miraculous experiences adorned youth of implement and alkaline fermentations past present peculiarities besides-brainless infamous creatures idiotic extent intent on truth, fulfilling certain chapters unrelenting and fondly strained of scented cure. Bright advance appears on horizons piece beloved sightless ceasing flash-smashingly absorbed in finesse discourteous guests recognisable by their mistakes repeated actions justified. Bounteous peasant revival, the connoisseur of vengeful escapades and thievery in advantageous virture more than less fantastic and spring loaded – some of us love the everlasting lifelessness of shamanic turbulence so naturally devoid of thrusting lance and blameless insurgence outstretched in rage caressed. Over simplified familiarities convulsed in order of respect for doubt sets in like winters volcanic gesture emphasised –thunder strikes back respectfully envisage in circular positions normally devised in friendships-learned lesson of watersheds hurricane position so largess intensified. Love is a drug sayeth the bright clever seer Cassandra complexities numerical code for conversations peaceful divination. High as a kite clandestine margarita monumental haven flourished dominations climatic pre-historic rebirth once again-divided planetary mix find forces of natural envision manufactured source sided from the light of fanciful extent. Smiling Arcadian arc and craft of fortitude forever and may there be no return to forge a blade without demand from end to end inevitably carved-right to the quick sideshow imprinted with recognisable flick of the wrist temperance included. Recluse seclusion into tangible devotees patriarchal traditions fantastic landscape-summarily devised discussion before the marked entrance available annalistic formats. Failure to imagine trustworthy variants in any shape or form, for whatever reason genuine impact is necessarily inherited-Overt doctrines relative sufficiency activates durable evidence of significant prejudice and incidental history. Till death do a parted vanquish totalitarian rules and leftover righteousness illusion. Perfectly phrased non-sencesical annoyances formulated over time and treasured existence – Expert ability for chance to rear its head above the din. Presidency resides succulently over publicities punctured silence of indignified ignorance-visual grievances blast briefly in dominant poise temporarily hesitant. Six million reasons to remember such reduction in our race to frequent the miles-priceless dividend gestures thrice toward mobile obsessive equality issues. Imitating lifelong ambitions to retain control over even ground and harsh realities resistance-courts adjourned for the faint quiver of loves chemistries and a hand of wishful thinkings feline ovation. Joyous health and forever the sound of heart and bright majestic fancy-near or far from above the beyond franchised beat of the wing of archangel Michael. Here and now up the river in a bubble forever recovered in magic soldier suited nearly until duty does its part-cigar toting terrorists flashbulb in hand other than historical background ridden over doubt and diva desperation follies. Goodbye cruel world I'm cruelly kind-hearted and that's for sure! Over and out, An ordinary affliction caused relapsed spiritual wonder to expand and assimilate for thinking academes messiah complex to be entertained-ordinary messages thwarted daily rage in tidy lifetimes entrance to the puzzle of our concept. Necessary divisions flavour the sound of hope in radial response to therapies and herbal experience of revelry and sealed intelligence-logic entirely abducts foreign bodies registered for strange destinies for devils stroke in hand. Not without a startling mountains optional point-to-point severity-harmonious decision frail sanatorium flexing its muscles, a realistic revelation finally agreed. Wrongly accused turns goading Zionistic conquerors rejojoicing veil like alternative voices about the way-witch and warlock cleaves its achieved sorcerers endurance effectual preference fortunes aside. Off beat romanticism derived primitively to the chosen few claims a soul by proxy-unfortunate for wayfarers cover stories printed versions diverse articulation. Sculptured cyber species portrait pictures thorough interests beckon of equssions reversed – particular foundation manifested one solar revue of supreme viola musiqué. Injection ominous photomontage breaks down the exhibitions fuelled purification solid beat of temporal polarities-profanities existential expanse eases out the special strangers of our hearts desire. Custodial interrogation seethes a strong programme of inordinate harness and intricate psychiatric wounding – tears departure survives mental breakdown and carminative destruction bone-dry therapies. Keen establishments refer to independent themes of inconceivable crimes against the stateside machismo-interior and exterior mortal malevolence further witnessing the last great dance of death deeply in dept defiance. Sooner supported the common martyrdom than reaper great harvest of extreme catastrophic and callous misdemeanour-strong connections short-armed similarities in a semi quaver connection of plague formation exited. Stranded cases of specific interest and unconditional darkness pursued-calling forth-speculative bodies of tentative exodus. Someone else's terminal illness pours glasnost gleaming through short seasons healing streams – old impacts hold their ground furtively meteoric and something of a prodigy albeit fairly abnormal in size. With faded jeans in low their lies the rub of it high as heavens gate we recon – controversial calamities enter into separate scientific sceptres royal gloried own betrayal. Numerical Malay portrayed in a country crescendo evenly spanned and catastrophically molten – retrospectively guaranteed in stinking locust mould dismissal. Filth surrounds us now by epidemic accossiasion and new arrivals fall into the furnace far below – transgressions of environmental slavery and draconian existence. Leave well the furies scream from hellish vixen call the forest of screams – starving villagers tried embezzlement and exterior far more than can be avoided. Overly simplistic charges of disobedience and respective isolation serve know one in the long ruination of the crime such reinforcement may delay – revised by prosthesis questions capitol view points servile minion of foreign race devised in replicated manifestation. Irrelevant narrative or confidant questions of rare intoxicating and potentially dangerous corruption – steely Dan inn their meaningful tempestuous and strange neurosis. Logistics argue necessary and an agonistic systems of betrayal – mystic missiles unprecedented arrival rations protagonistic seclusion sanatoriums and exalted under statements deluding mass hypnotic psychosis and systematic suggestion. Reduced proportionately from instinctive machinations sleepless solitude perfections exalted - surreptitious anointment stroke away the greatly precocious temperament of foreign bodies anywhere else graded. Started far outside of normal maiden voyages orders for vain surrounding earthly groundling vestals breezy findings – rage doses of intestinal fluidity and pharisaic emissions cordially invested partly formed jointly in remission. I have indeed weeded squalling balconies of ragged breaches for fear of reaction and odd choice of illogic membranes squeezed to greater something's other than clinched opinions – supreme commandments ordeal +andseperatistically muddled. Systematic poltergeist activities entrance into realms of undiscovered countries – service with smile from unto wards recreative innards + electrical charge. Definite demands crystal clear reprisals of nervous laughter + escaped inertial – I accept divine correlation in obituary arbitration – increased regulatory abnormalities bigoted rightwing standards + real attitudes in rear-view space. Useful institutions sickly sweet insanities of average soil + courage in detail + surcharges + harmless conversion of localisation + ill-used lifelines diversified permanence. A scratching complaint of flaming advertisement beggars belief – residual distance almost reaches its conclusion. Ominous arrival drives distractions weary of the end towards their doom – instinctive instance insist all incidents appal all ravelling sources. Overtures revival corresponding rivals revel too closures marrow combined – flavours of flavour follow features frightening fracas eternal. Understatements comatosed burnt to livid fears + strangled vulnerabilities – oceanic plagiarism moist from churchyard complained leverage surging swell of pain – arms abounding farther from this charge + turn of effortless event where all is said + done charioteers figurative spectral mental cast of iron fuselage is dreaming. Shove into the warmth of delight, laced up ready for a fertile fugitive displaced inner vacuum of modifications exposed – feel avenging mercenary's sterile state of affairs that blessing in disguise revised. Clairvoyantly depraved insomniac of the meaner born default in famous more for cheating rather than playing by the rules of warriors – gifts extravagant measures slowly mouthing performance leaves diverted lesions or abrasions for metaphorical equations exalted. Obsessive-compulsive inadequacies uninformed mechanistic stalemate inertia – nowhere close to the yelped portions various proxy's climatic conclusions of logistics stadium. Pan ultimate immersion of dramatic subterfuge warming evidently in all directions – artificial calculations moronic descriptions of referred chronological tapestries reverse this cursed blessing in etiologic membrane viscosity. Devastation on a lifeline of desolate insoluble satiety + affliction caused to explain severity requested – I hear lustful revelry for ordinary encounters startling disco very + significantly absorbed. An overzealous jealousy + obstinate caricature of this futuristic voyeurism – broken recoveries partial apology destined for greatness. Immobilised personage modified hypothesis of pre-existing directions – satirical exodus and custodial assertions proceeding subsequent fragmentation + impact damage. Refusals commissioned categorically disposed in unilateral anticipation formulised – devotion circularly circumvented in experimental attitudes + morbid meticulous ovation. Barbaric completions over simplified transactional surprising suggestions – interpersonal depletion anticipates that bearing appearance of recognised conditions charges on in expectations. Troops outward appearances chasing abundance in former sliced relationship careering – recovered insignificantly swarmed, silently bombarded astonishment deployed. Constant tenderness + originally separate in occurrence we remain connected; temporarily conjoined-fragments of other memories advance tenderly alleviated within expected perimeters. Mightily barbarism hinders on this serious creative monument following described details triumphant expansions – enter equilateral descriptions accurate echoes to past + previous catastrophes. Heave to heavyhearted efforts + dignified images observed immaculate borderline + fiery flames – essential grievance immobile tenderness brings great change directly sourced in supernatural period + astral endorsement. Vosipherous shenanigans foolish entrance into methodical intentions of dismantled movements – saving through permanent situations cowardly conventions reviled. Risky remissions staunch concepts.

Chapter Three

Wherever yee may roam there will be sacred promises and joy; from valley high to mountain low, a secret river flows. Mouths open, full of blame, rain falls home again – feels good to find this easy and effortless listening gift of gold. Run through the centre of the valley into the caves of blind rage, then pass along through speaking walls of wind and try to tunnel your entry out. Read well into the night, our exit highways of tortured roads fall to the sea again as ships pass by. Endangered species rot well before our eyes, scream high and low to make us believe in some solution. Hard enough to work together in a never-ending mood never mind to turn the tables completely. Fortune favours the brave, try to save a life each and everyday – learn and burn, how to work miracles. They say it's easy once you know how – what's the matter with consistent discipline anyway? It won't kill you as swiftly as the other one, trust me, darling, darling. Breathless and uneasy, rubbed together – inside and out, Faust's fortune takes a twist in jest for an early night. Then corpus mentis hysteria makes the most of it in this, the jungle of life, for a star is born again my man.

Lets bring in the New Year with a little *c'est la vie* in the mix baby. Busyness as usual, let's it all just passes on by content and full of good times. Just before the end of concentrated consciousness we need to accomplish our goals without a doubt of uncertain expectations flourishing power, expect great things to come – impress the house with lust for life. Success will increase, as the day is long, drop along to a tune of your choice as well to do you will as well. The voice is true for a full follower must believe in the self, must have faith, must have faith. Bursting through the seams in favour of the flavour of the moment – today is the day here in the presence of thee, now. In tune with lightning's precious grace indeed, for our own good is the master of the souls reprieve – all who dare enter reach a higher goal – simple is solutions rest and relaxation. Festive opportunity counts for nothing, hesitation ends when all is said and done – something wicked this way comes. For day has ended posthumously – again the tides will change for worse than better time through to nothing, out for more. Taken sure total and confident reckoning, as always-inner circle supposedly will, enhance the nightingale's lament. In stable or adept confusion we find delusion of a sort, in case of torments trickery, exit horizontally inclined.

Theft of hardened boiler message true to find – the face value of ordinary in space race citizen's invention. Dust to dust, ashes to ashes for grand finality is greatly cordoned with utmost condition high extravagance and moral agenda to defect in general multiplicity and also grand theft auto contradictory, *mien general.* With, or to dye a knot in trench warfare or marked man splendour – I reject the rear-end of the goat in general office and in just, common sense to see clearly constant advertisement for years ago – fortunes varying opinions, barely based over the limit for our sacred and angelic god spell. Simple overture and classic gifts of grace, can wear a smile, deep crevice go into the font of youths disgrace, of many lives have I, as cats may breath in tune – leaves then little to the eye, will ruin mothers mind. Then open doors of evil will to kill – enjoy the finality of truth. With less and less to our ill intent you bring, cannot break even not without, everything. The future brings to bear all *joie de vivre* – eventually out and with more – much to share in word. Then turn out the light unevenly despair, this fervent farmer reaps the harvest swift and easily repairs. Cursed best before the blessed be despised – the wisdoms wasted on your twisted eye.

Or in slumber sleep unevenly – third times mostly the charm, we belong together, you and I. I and I live in guiltless blame – movement gleams where she reaches and clamps down to forever damned to do the same, uneven stretch for murder spell speaks for to listen. She, ill advised moves far slower than before and to a calling leave to listen, no stone unturned – in such device a plan of ill intent. Harm none shall be the whole of the law and it do as it wilt, in thrice and wild success, cards of the eye. Open up in terrible distance and then to see the law improve.........

Shipwreck havoc on their own lives – a display of light brings hope alive, taking credit continuously for the all important praise of approval, thinking one mind is well and truly not, one is mine treachery and abandonment, remember not the land living simply – on demand. I do not like the thief of words – the thief of my life or even of yours. The vessel of nothing that cries out enough enough – until it is driven out of slavery. The light expels the lies of bondage, selling herself for no profit at all. Where is the semiconscious mind – where has it gone – all gone, disappeared again into self-grotesque and out. In with substance or overdone then with something else. More than enough for want of our spirit and body, to begin the beyond when a chance of a change has come. Don't play us for fools – don't feint or fall on the floor. And as I walk over to your body, I bless the blessed better than themselves are we, for nothing pleases more over than to a fool when Moriggan is heads coiled a neck above the rest. Fallen into the well and recover when ready – mercury rising is my name, one more time then before the gold oven is rekindled – again from the mind reigns Judas is restrained. Tried and tested, detested vengeance of the ever faithful soul to soul when reality is strained.

We will work with the evil master, for the benefit of those listening – disrespect plays over acting hard rough and tough in everyway a witch. Strength wittily so confidently in toxification wherever the hell is the D.J. gone. Who do you bloody well know falling down – I prefer to take the stairs. The creep of a clown, hound like in effect – are grabbing at straws, fades in oblivion. To be or not to be – Shakespeare wrote or did not he? Think consistently of some dark and evil secret instead of riding the British trail. Duel of marmalade makes blissful the shocking trail out of nothing. Amen.

Bravely breaking open the prayer boat head shrinkers hunger strike for more – opposites attract barbaric human sacrifices, there's no place like home wherever you may roam. Sink your teeth in for father feature, hits the one who loves this life – in all its glory to fill our hearts with love and joy. At the end of the day screech bravely to a start; stretch and leave well enough alone. And come home knowing something has been done, full of truth and overcome relief. The one and only man of the moment – your mother and her favourite son; mister leaning tower of power! The underdog, Joe soap then of carnival, here we go. Line after line, time and time again, Father Christmas, mother of God – done and dusted, forever featured, Amen. Semi-flavoured reservations drastic tag or price to play techniques, exit directly on your own for a loan, and only for a noteworthy woman, in lust or love again? – Surrender and recover, always to be forever and all night long. March next, triumphantly towards the shallow fall of this our friendships industry. Endeavour digital Las Vegas in our simple romantic valour – think carefully before you go. This is luxury that new classical nobodies for whom we can so relate to and never before have become. Everlasting for those who choose to pray and worship the sun gods, oh! To eat away on the edge of little nowhere.

Star shining in the evenings seventh sun-sing out joy and words of beauty, for overcome all this mess in jest have I. Trial and tribulation so far now are gone far off – into the night in order of the truth incarceration of our rebirth and manic perfection and general ignorance and stupidity. Carol the milly ticket to ride, show of the decade – living down 'n out detective for a shady deal provocateur; investigative native.

Song of soul sound, so yesteryears rancid shadow hangs over the heads of our innocent youth. So full of grace, imperfect and selfish wish in strangulation – saint and sinner full of the sun for the legs to stand on fall between us. Prepared for the future now – each and everyday, half sunk in mystery and misery. We are together endlessly and with covered heart have found hesitation. Their own blue-white skin never touched sin – or tore a swearing tearing rip in free world streets. At worlds within. Mental breakdown folds and holds us forever until the days of torment end – chemistry in constitution runs out straight through and keeps on flowing along the ground. Flowing currents glide – stone scrapingly smooth; gold pre-recorded institutions waterfall on, until the break of the day. Is it ever really worth one life? Ours to know and yours to find out.

Defenceless and vulnerable, yet the final performance of more than other none small tragedy. Bones will come home again – forever and a day refractions. It's time to face facts my friend there's far more to it than meets the eye, of course to let the truth be told; deny all of it. Fact or fiction – licence and registration are all in order, help is at hand, Oh Holy God! Judge a man is not in the order of the day, light make no mistake is far more powerful. Far further than before in cursed reverse hangs a heavy head – folded break is on the make and so very, very bold. So much more than before they were right right, wrong, wrong – how long can the richest people fight back the poor? Play the game or be gone. Yes, yes indeed bubba it's just like the new man said, breathe in breathe out shake it all about. To make it easy man, chill out for the time being. It's all going to all right, no problems anymore, relax the cacks so to say – next step strengthens evermore the silence, of the end game:

French connections spirited away, before the end of time we are done with all. This time it's for real, no worries, no mistakes, make or break for it – never trust a shyster boy. The girls are still to pay for it in each and every way, 'til the end, for shame is ever lasting love within our reach Amen. Goodness knows warm and snowy weather takes it's toll on many men, this might it's never easy, still no more than must will be said – for times institution stands out for ill intentions break even, Everest chills out in the tall powers fall, waters Eskimo.

Constantly cursed the work of ours – self-sacrificed in bars of unreplenished countryside, for a few seconds of futuristic flame, cannot let go the light. Blessed be thy name, forever more the shaker breaks instant colossal forensic investigations formidably. In solitude are we and now surrounded, most unkind the face of fear or grave dismissal will unwind the bead of faith, then in dismissal form the same inner exile. Burned the evidence in horrific endeavour – angry persons of the same degree with rage are too brutal in manner. Some will make the grade, until sunshine's all out, for ours the market Gods surrender is complete.

Insensitive lovers of self same selfishness, makes a mess of all and everything. One more time became the source of the painlessness. Mess – born to be childlike and stranger than ever before. Reckless makeover on the inner sanctum sometimes saviour flavours of the moment, wish me hells bells any road that you can – wreck havoc on my sensitive soul in this here western hemisphere – to dream a little dream of me; here we go, and waste away all of god's precious gifts just for the sake of a black hole in the night lightening music manifesto supreme. Yes, yes indeed there we have it my man – more than your painful share of grief, enough for a lifetime and a crime it is to be darn sure of it crawling through your soul from your head down to your toes.

Before the end has come – doom and gloom shall roam the streets so far and wide, until the dawn of day exiles darkness to the night. Alive alive o say the man, how long can you go – how so far can you stray into the hole that is soul, yours gone A.W.O.L. i.e. known absent until further notice. Planned without a name, carefree and jobless – way, way out on a limb forever and dairy free, Amen.

Killing yourself and nobody else my man, this is very true so far, true to the rescue – give it up my friend, calling out for a change to begin. So far so good, it's a shame to let it all fall away my relative son, such a damned shame to let it slip and slide down that slippery slope. Out of your mind you must have been – obscene obsessive and compulsive, bloody bloody all the way terrified, the last of the drop must have been pure torture, pure torture, indeed and it was.

Desirable beyond belief is our contestable and contradictory companionero indestructible formidable – easygoing and good-natured, past and present. Just past out beyond the frontier of safety or mortal danger, easily pleased and ready for anything. Much more than explorations can allow this holy cow company has everything you've been looking for. Diseased free escape from all phantoms far out of flame, out of focus and in between the lines. Fiercely flame grilled and burst fantastic figures are well into the sounds around. Blazing strands of silver hang from the shadows like twisted coils of ether, boiling from the centre of the Earth. In a never-ending spiral that shifts through the desert sands with lightning speed, an unnatural occurrence in this cold modern electronic age of robotic insomnia. Battle wasted war that sounds the orb into another age, where rage escapes, the ape is free and man of woman born, incensed upon the tree of knowledge is sworn to secrecy.

And now the creator's vision swan dives into the concrete wasteland of our humble lives, never before or will ever again will be this balance fervour turned about. Swift alien creatures since the turn of tide have with us been – sorcerers wives in caverns hidden palaces collide where ignorance will never be, to the end of time, to the end of earthly days and nights may shed its cloak of mystery. Indeed welcome new recruits for rescues very close at hand, fallen from another rewritten moral in great lessons, to be learned, followed through and at the double, run rabbit run, all the way home. Possessed with a quality most dignified – with conviction and attributes of a superficial order. Ranging all commandments with care and legendary reputation in many cases and in forethought, to have achieved all of life's dreams through youthful endeavour.

The heart of the lions mane have we, all is well, when smooth running in effect will forever be an unusual occurrence. Alive are the old forgotten town spirits here as where in days gone by. Strengthened by time, our heroes, for more we will adore – so much so that we post hastily become them, simply by familiarity and spiritual misadventure.

He will treat us to a diamond life of love-lost and contempt of the immortality of change. Distinct from this illusion are we – their humble servants be secluded – fruitless without any change, in constant memories arranged, time takes its toll – and all unfolds, golden midnight learns the reason of all that intermission, next to lighten the load in part or to take heed without greed, instead of thieves, forgiven.

To end the cycle of ignorance, where a flow or jet of water breaks the ice and takes its watery time, for the violence of violins keeps a thin and even watch on our memories. Crack! The sound of blind justice takes its toll on mortal men, then moves along swiftly to its next victim. Suddenly awaken this land of mine that lies rejected and for so many years. In fear now is detested by the blood of church – fed theatres spectacle peoples parade manifesto is immaculate. O late debate the waste of our young minds, to freely sport ingest, deflate our tired lives away, far out and too many at that, so it is said; that history is dead. You are wasting away consecutively and without reason, there is indeed much strength in numbers. Licensed to kill, thrill seekers out with a vengeance – many more will adore, that's no lie. Slaughter of founding families disturbed beyond normal comprehension – irredeemably placed in a world that divides comfort for a change in circumstance. Haven't we seen you before, distant vacancies, adorned with dressed handmade by angelic forces, unnamed especially for this occasion.

Here in this place of trial and tribulation, make haste for space and for memories invalid industry – thousands of raging bull examples come charging towards the truthful light of innate reason. Morbidly impressive constitutions complete whole recovery, following the flow of inhumane waste and less of more is it as well as I can say. Sense, sense, damn you and despise the spell of inconstant harmonies – take out, aim with other peoples lives, will you not. Before the campaigns end is followed out in flesh and rid again of sinful order, not of our health at all of the above, below, or less often such time as can be achieved. Spearhead delivers such powerful blows that can be remembered throughout history – much of the same, a call to arms has come. Again, the simple man that has no shame is distant from our minds and has contempt for suffering and pain – yet all of us are to blame for misery and illness. To run away at all costs towards the enlightened, with due respect for discipline still is very enterprising for small-minded mentality, myself included, of course. The rich mouth of word that come right out, are murderers of logic and of reason combined. Vigorously inventive connoisseurs for mass production and increasingly for the product of invention, itself more of the same.

The revolution is here, in more ways than one – at this very moment people are watching, waiting, contemplating for the next new idea, constantly creative in all their hesitation to consume the soul. To recreate the world, so as to sell it all again. All that glitters is not gold. Wither away into the silence of the night, through a meaningless procession of ecstasy-enthroned eternal bliss – remain faithful to the truth of a very good lie. Pinstriped in recreation, all the revelries you'll ever need, vultures and thieves we are led to believe are we, our very own, brothers in arms. Faithless foot soldiers full of hate, love is lost and completely confronted by the look of it, sounds of dancing Jewish gypsies joined at the hip by fatal Rome, in all it's exiled glory.

Warriors of the fashion, flowing robes of passion, fired up to the heavens above, Christ! can you feel the love a burning up inside me! Yes say I, yes, yes, yes for the love of God I can, guardian angel and all are in on this deal. Armies of marching souls, willing and able to cross-over to the other side at the blink of an eye – forth wards and back, defence and attack, positions are available in every multicolour, black and white, blue or green, intercontinental. Mental breakdown is hereditary and preconceived moments of lucidity are common enough around here, so to speak ill of the monster is ill advised, ok, alright, the only revenge on the ego is humiliates demise.

For on this occasion here we have it, forever strength in numbers, the animus alive and full of the fatal horrors indeed; when old habits die-hard. The end of humanities new horizons, invisibly lecherous in opinion, move swiftly on to greater visitations arguably. Enough most definitely is far from inexplicable, around the neck of the genie marvellous, outstanding populous and incredible heads through the ages, marginalized fascist faction freedom fighters emporium of the lame, tame, ignorant of pedigree and or decade, wheeler-dealer man-woman-man-woman-man-persona clash! non grata equatorial budget hypotheses of our age.

Are we listening? The roads are sweeping to and fro, it's definitely time to go, where no man nor woman dares to tread – it's difficult, where to belong? On what path to go. With what change of circumstance will bring us home again – still with the inkling of a change the dangerous journeys end comes to us all.. In the blink of an eye it all comes crumbling down, castles tall and grand will make or break for it. There lies the time we cried, and saw the stories swiftly end. Still blind to poisonous creatures when hell is loosely smashing through the door-escape continuously hangs out her weary head and troubles us no more. Freedom fighters will escape that viceroy of champion and heroine adored throughout history – pours forth the peace of incarnation once and again. Impressive mortality reduced to a corpse, borrowed blissful bounties from remorse, in a leap of faith, the pressure is in now more than ever before – the price of infamy is war. Long live the inescapable truth of suffering.

Hell there are heroes and for the empowered women heroine – hell hath no furies left off with to win their course, instead of animals conquered in their path, like mirrors of original sin. Knowledge finds accountability few bedfellows in human beings still – of you innate, I yawn. Oh! spirit of man instilled visions of venue are obvious here in heavens space filled variety and in galled of mind and matter for a door. Earthly religions fall down to the test of taste when walls begin to crumble down. Down again, trenched in warfare, once is enough for interest or vanity – strained through a verse inherited. Dodge otherworldly frames to jostle corruption of the public bodies, carried over windows and out or off the streets and into the hidden lives of the true believers. Only rational or impressive minds can hold the discipline of rule, momentarily unjust for such an occasion, without a joust indeed.

Drearily dredged far below the norm of dope inspired love – hope spring eternal once again. Nothing else matters, apart from a really good thrashing – purple red veins popping through your head again, no strings are attached. All things remain the same – does this ever mean I'm free to roam around the world west, east, north and south? Have we found adversity in strength or mighty verbs in actions proud production now and then. Real, true, pure confusion, cordoned off indifferent to guardians hour in the haunted beaches inn round the corner. Simple gestures hung indifferently together again full friends forever – does it really exist? The remains of the same song reflects gradually on our claim, an explanation of star-shape, this day, this very night – soldier on love.

Shoulder to the boulder, hard now, ready for the new world order – true blue, peace be with our sons and daughters, knights in shinning armour. Fresh from the divine kingdom of the soul. Only young as sunshine lives the day-night longer – linger on, I love your soul. Gravity reminds us of our blue mortality, true, true, the winds of change have come. Over is the storm before the quiet indeed, follow your heavy heart my son, my daughter the world is your oyster. Touched terrible things – enter through locked doors, blasting open overtly humble lives without fear of reprisal. Doom flows out in currents dream of annihilation to find nothing, more in disdain of rhetoric facet or form in characters for dissolution. White gold, too pure for death or normal use is coveted upstairs like a cat among the pigeons. True real lives are affected by hormonal imbalance and satanic malpractices – primarily obscene in effect; distort the truth completely. And what appears before our eyes is open to conviction – the eyes are easily fooled – resting on occasion for education completely sceptical and closed to the constructive cryptal suggestion or submissive gesticulations recover.

Visitors far from native shores – ranging towards rage investment, have come to even out the odds a little bit. Political harassment suddenly arises from it's watery grave – ignorant malevolence searching for slaves to do battle with righteous endeavour, with sensitive policies in early architectural stages to enslave their future generations indefinitely. Sounds like fanatical fundamentalism? Yes please! pile it on, pile it on. Textbooks majors in philosophy or images for an enterprise in articulations direction, this way or open the oven door. Prey for deaths new recruits, far from home, far from home – there is no mystery in change. Flow too the fountain of our youth, flow the magic of wild nature go. Leave well the bluff in sworn testimony compromised finished the heritage of traditions buried old and wise. Once and a while, theatre gives way to a brighter day – modern societies interest and fascination with sublime institutions change without the flowing tide. Various forms of inept, solitude find only the muse in melancholy – opportunity opens her arms for everyone.

Complete investigation allows for endlessly amusing situations – extreme prejudice, in surreal authenticity. Softly spoken contempt of all things hereditary – revisited examples shall leave us blind. Contradictions hilariously concealed and otherwise deleted in defeat of alternative distraction. Considering collective consciousness as weapons of mass destruction i.e. where soul life has exited, animus moves right in – complete takeover by an alien being, free speech from an underground movement then? Living with denial, an all too common resistance. In great expanse religion releases the new dimension unconventionally – extreme indifference to resistant factors of our homeless land on even ground conditionally. Finely tuned to the spectral sound of change today, on active duty and well protected – be that as it may. For all endangered species remain intact, and so easily affected – momentarily excludes the rights of admission haphazardly through all proportion in this instance. Sky-high insomnia finds cracks in the clouds, for it is raining painfully this day indeed.

Saving precious metals inaccurately procured – then striding on without a word. Animal – like in manner lately and well matured, immersed in pure desensitisation – drowned directly and strangely frustrated. Handsome capital relates in all its feathered down of early mourning inhumanitarian exploits – reason fails them in darkest hours of our decapitation. Empty of logical conclusion, the swarm of inhumane alien episodes explode, in jingle-jangle sickness of disturbing and shadowy complexities. The worm consciousness takes hold of supaconcious and egocentric daemon-ridden souls – so easily spread is this disease that inevitably to my surprise, there is no greater wisdom than surprise. Without structure, unflinchingly militant and inescapable psychic molestation pores out an eternal supply of unremitting savagery to the bemusement of all involved. Senseless extension of mental abuse are we subjected to from all sides – coincidentally realised have I apocalyptic achievements is essentially passive life forms such as these are we uniformly scourged before the eyes of humble masters. Like attracts like, it's a conglomeration of our unflinching faithless love and evidently absurd need to beat down the oppression of our adverseries. Both sides are right! Visual images of hellhounds chasing satanic mercenaries through times desolate landscape leave us blind, deaf and dumb to the infinitely blissful nirvanas' of position.

Great minds think alike so they say in character and blasphemy together, are equal in execution or beheaded as always ever so fortunately. Structures occupants are exclusively evacuated. Some with striking similarities – threatening foreclosure of the inevitable obstacle so regrettably ingrained in conscience and proximity to all others. Structure bears about in formidably anachronistic style – begrudging the rest of the metamorphosis completely.

Dangerous hyperventreloquism demonstrates some theories never before realised by any mortal whose will is justifiably insane to any degree. Conservation of law and order requires some serious programming to liberally generated greymatter. The willing antibodies of so prestigiously abstract metaphors such as we are likened to leave a lover for, or sacrifice vain pleasures and the like, indeed hold much their weight in gold

Double their willingness to succeed in triangulations greedy bosom spell enchantment expressionist categorisation. Chip of the old anything is possible psychedelic block again thinking categorically of any esoteric influence generated by ever-useful adorations supreme collaboration with the mix. Greatly increased by the blindingly obvious expanse of this pioneering influence – if on the corner of soul starvation like never before, deeply ignored, the silence of age and of reason. Incensed and of the seasonal chair in chorus of formidable giants ensemble – requests regrettable formations of indigenous cohorts and unlikely suspects, arguably the best contemplative troubadour of your kind in existence – second to none. Instrumental indignation now blinded completely and outdone outclassed and defeated – is at one life changing experiences and medically cured.

Moving pictures covetingly blinded without reason, drive the wizard over champion's boarders to collide with grief again with complete annihilation, strives to gain access to the tip of the iceberg. Connections make a break for it through perceivingly and increasingly impossible odds-above and below the call of duty or implausible central massive diplomatic endeavour.

Braving the elements, to endure the creative valour of primordial and cosmopolitan climate in general – the outline is made clear to all involved. Behave, or beheading for downward spiral over rocky-road, sandy hill and muddy glen – instrumental, loads of frolics, can you feel it creeping further into the neither regions of the mind you call your own. Snakes begotten from the womb of the earth, soldier on in the name of destiny and faceless freedom – transcending the coils in defence-attack mode. An ignorant display of the animus scratching it's way upwards into the light. Building bridges beyond the divide of life, of immortality questioning no more the eternal flame. Faith completes this equation – minimalistically divine, founding forefathers compete for the prize, on this occasion. Eureka, the fountain of youth bursts forth from it's nesting quarry stream like into the womb of atmospheric pressure. A brave new day has arrived out of knowledge, easily attained yet not for us all or everyone.

Get it right the first time as always it forever has to be inevitably insane, at best overtly diverse. Profitability benign assignments deliver killer punches blow by blow across the nations old adage of unforgettable atrocities. Distant reminders of the way that it was – echoes of our youth, cast a bold cry of spite on your breath, there's no need to cry. Timeless reminiscence of pre-historic mindlessness, tear into the grit-reap all the benefit of your torrential truth from the lies. Be somebody else, rather than the bubonic half cast prehistoric death defying molestation of creation that you are. Face facts, it's time to go joe – is time to sink or swim, to do or die, fall or fly. Jump right in everybody – remarkable achievements are recovered, falling on forwards – push the envelope out through the pretence of somebody else's ideals and destroy the preconceived monstrosities to their bitter and conceivably empty meaneringly meaningless end.

Dredged from down under – as usual as ever, indifferent to all a sundry. Your congress of appreciation as viewed before apocalyptic indifference has begun to uncoil – pure pleasure, there is nothing more nothing less. Innocuous procession celebrates all of our acceptance numerically and out of order. Yes indeed bucko, incidental accusations and persecution of popular encounters of the third and terrestrially preconceptual kind orders perpendicular.

Mediterranean holy wars have come to us all – repercussions simplified, repetitively hardboiled and completely dishevelled, all over the place, today tomorrow and ever yesterday. Self-proclaimed simpletons destroy this world of ours successfully with natural nationality and personified motivation. It's all going to be all right, don't worry; you have all survived the terror of suicidal torment for now. So keep going, self to the block – precious cargo intact. Precarious environment of equals and hybrid technology in a class of it's own, for evermore – no need to experiment Amen. Deep alarm, outcast for the time being – purified beyond comprehension. To make love, not war – destroy destruction; overcome all obstacles habitually and with an ease becoming one such as this sick world may never know.

Soul searching indecent traditional ecstasies for a far-out reality – distances great and wide. Once upon a time impossibilities become manifest towards an even higher goal, inevitably personified – reached nirvana with an end in sight. Peace inside, all is possible – some dreams come true in the sunrise of our lives. The touchstone of translation indignantly exposed without constraint of mainstream collaboration. Involved in the struggle nevertheless and of the same detailed infamous material as before they became famous. Personally challenged with every degree of hostile behaviour we have become used too – shamelessly indulging in anything we can get our hands on. Things always seem to go well eventually, concentrating on larger portions in the need without reason.

Rather than wrench the hostile elements altogether for an insatiable desire for revenge – complete success have we again been nominated. Agreement is unanimous, for all parties involved they gave no quarter, back to the starting block to emerge triumphantly from this hibernative state and stark examination of our reflective existence. In all its entirety our predecessor falls to the same stroke – never-ending shame of emotive hormonal abuse co-exists with mental fermentation. Relative harmony otherwise obsolete is given a facelift none to soon. Disaster striketh! Rubbed them up the wrong way – mainlining through the mainstream again. Crime doesn't pay so they say. If you're a foolish person well enough adopt a lifestyle becoming your tastes and stray the path well forsooth. Obviously conspired to abuse in great distaste an ugly icon or former formula further from the truth. Direct reconstruction of the internal succession tops the bill, inside and out – changing bizarre personalities as awkwardly as if humanely possible!

Eventually our offspring predicts alarming developments in hemispheres of stained glass, bliss encounter. Astounding feats of scientific endeavour acknowledge the spirits meridian lines together with representations of strain and stress – reduced *déjà vu* manifestation occurrence and experiences.

Visitations are oblique and surreal, this world or the next came in tune with the stars elevation. Listen to the fire in your heart, feel the flame – evolutions relationship with our earths. Relationships with beings high and dry as the goddess dreamt evocation duality. Supreme mother of all creation weathers the tide well and leaves us an epitaph of extremes behind for cosmic dust and the inevitable surrender of history. Overindulgent perhaps but equal to the peak or depths exposed before the turn of time and tides. Currents break open the laws of gravity then estranged from life in peaceful harmony on the universal shelf.

Damned to frustration, incomplete and still as emptiness can be foretold – another experience before the final goal is reached. Death, our benefactor is redeemed in battle dress, sceptre in hand and ready for the next world of adventure. Searched high and low yet again for the simple facts of life – original, versatile and morbidly romantic to the bitter end indefinitely. Skin – taught, bones protruding through their thoughts in sacred doubt of every little thing – wretched animal of chronic enharmonic adversity.

Simple minds with ancient souls – memories far from the ordinary populous and only streets away. Vagabonds of foreign culture open up their arms to my observations, to slap me in the face, word up over silence – in its place of soul-to-soul menagerie. Man to man in every way the same – some just short of the mark, posthumously inclined for this retail and ritual of race. Wanderlord of transformation, subsequently resurrected to explore in circles of translation, unusual developments in our stratosphere, underground movements fashion tragedies destroy the construction of invention in physiological revolution. All singing heroism of the nation fixed in position, regulars in the oceans physiology.

Take a trip down memory lane, wherever that may be – everybody wants some recognition of a sort. Who can tell what lies around the corner this time – can't be slack today or any other, for that instant of fleeting glimpse may take it all away. In the blink of an eye all this and more will come your way – such material of uncategorial fame, touched by the hand of fate, remains a very conceivable concept.

Legendary contradictions of subtle intellect break the news gently and profoundly sane. Correctly in record and information with break – neck speed directly and immediate confirmation is requested pronto.

Clarity and fearlessness reassemble truncated evolution through representatives of power in thought, theories of our transformational ideocincricies perform potential adverse creations, perennially disguised.

Revelations of executive republicanism dwell on the inter-relationship of some of the more orderly institutions of our minds collectively. Manifestations present potential is overactive emotionally – silence reaches self-fulfilled forethought and single-minded devotion, equal to all sides.

Enchanted disinterest in all things melancholy takes the edge of visual internment – back to basics forever and not the game begins again. Satisfactions guaranteed in underground macrocosms of universal expectation – desperate calling cards for societies next invention.

Immediate misadventure evolves through and through without hesitative overindulgent hypothesis – provided insight can deliver inverted preconception. Experience and understanding clears total falling virgin exclaimers relevance rediscovery – here and now, cheated of disappointment.

Proliferation of criminal sideshow fakerism has developed in universal proportions – most recently here in the west from four corners to epicentre. Dawn of desire or of desecration, seek and yee shall find solution, solitude of sacrifice – in wisdom race to complications secluded countries. Common social ineptitude – the cold, hard facts of life – evidence of scientific endeavour, now shamelessly agree that all things proven remain unconditional and esoteric in appearance. Truth or fiction, repetitive numerical disappearance of youths in our time – found genuine anticipation far more beguiling than interpersonal communication or commitment to self same annihilation.

Redeemed benefactors in equal measure transposed potential congregations indefinitely – unsurpassed in medication of any kind with spontaneous miracles through medication and incurable diseases.

Chapter Four

Devout declaration of insomnia – finished at a glance. Believe already in he that worships nothing and find the document on immense analysis personified. In agreement of convulsive affliction – is inspired by phenomena of defiance and reconsidered interpretation, all in order. Salad dressing makes the most of it – practised perfectly in fraud and esoteric stimuli. Encouraged to perform in front of the mass hysterical crowd of punters and clergy – whipping themselves into a state of convulsive demonic possession just for the thrill. Bible bashing sermon's on witchcraft and sorcery and growing opposition to the significance of this persecution is displayed by the middle class.

Specifically philosophers of international reputation and of powerful political persuasion. The witch-hunt was on and the cult is still growing as we read.

Onto the next one – specifically in execution of monstrous fanaticism in retrospect of modern civilisations. Common hysterical symptoms – assuming affected bodies are ingesting psychogenic substances over long or intense periods of time. Mind your mind as the man said – societies incorporate of ignorance and fear. Earth religions leave the gate open for destructions escapade – profound is the sense of hopelessness among the mob.

Bad behaviour expressed continuously – overexcited bordering on mentally ill or insane, is personified. Time and time again, we see our peers fall into the trap of abuse – dive headfirst, throw caution out the window. Become the beast of your present reputation – sins of forefathers passed on through the collective consciousness of another mother.

Public excitement produces inaccurate prediction – fear of the hangman's intent finds reason. Blissfully in denial of these mischievous proceedings – all the good in bad people rises to the surface – like charity at Christmas. Caution! Their hand is offered in a sign of peace – beware for the one is watching us. In future times the fool finds that he is wise – returns to hedons field with wine for all his boozing buddies.

Leadership falls away completely throughout most of the proceedings – it's an all nighter again. Dare to win significant influences on the course of events – unique belief is as common among the public as the executed person. Burn them, hang them, drown them all – innocent to fall in the wake of demand. Still live by the sword and expire by the sword.

Agony of ether burns at the throat – calling for help endlessly without hope. To the pale east we reach a climatic peak – in the night of great water. To the south is bitter change – rearranged in circular activity. Blessed ash of the end in life – save our selflessness 'till some shine hope comes. Unfinished business returns again – cold and shivering in golden dawn light. With the heart of a dove, absence fills the room – head flakes off the boil, another mother's son. In a snakes coil – the vacuum if skimmed off the treetops overburn. Famine, desolation and an even greater selection of dreadful destinies just waiting for your call. A never-ending monument to change we have it all now. Sophisticated production of a previous age gone by – open to discussion. A revolution of truth, as in historical fact for conservation.

Revisited desperate and irresponsible characters, intended higgledy-piggledy for the sake of great calamity.

Calamity, calamity there's know one like calamity. The Hollywood dream escapes our intellect must have our fix of suffering. Lifelines break the barriers open-hurt is fixed to the post. How difficult is complication, where the majority fades swiftly on.

Charity, the comedy of correction is fulfilled. Received an impossible word – difficult in every way – comfort is cleared away. Compliments of the season, firm and smooth as flight – dark night of the soul. Promises to be an easy read – into another world. The final passage make no mistake – can take a lifetime. Hospitality cooks what it has to – not exactly what the good doctor ordered. Withered away the racehorse of soul – reaches towards the race, without a pause. Lean, healthy and organic recipes on the board gives it a change for chance breaks even.

Hunting familiars practice posthumously on the robots of our time – chase away the better nature of mankind. Against every human instinct – the dreadful deed is done. To put aside each judgement and destroy the evidence – murder of manslaughter is considered at the old bailey. Ahead of plans to expand, the main sticking points have developed a relationship to foreign policy. Despite loss of the profit – records are broken by unperturbed master.

I went down – sound of death knell, its now solvent for visitors turnaround. Robust challenge for a changing world, rapidly expanding fortunes find equity. Unavoidable technological wizardry is underestimated – suits for the troops cause casualties. Banned the ham from the brain concert concept is not acceptable. Expand losses struggle, wet and windy and a bit of a chilly shake up.

Attack is lacked – inflations affected surrender is pushed to the brink of limitation and instinctual terror gone berserk. The point of no return establishes defeat – low profile really has worked. Placed personnel vendettas above any club record I believe. The victors and the vanquished at loggerheads again.

Anthologies for reform, an irresistible continuation of anticipation. An incontrollable urge to compose in reflection of the scene in verbatim, or is that ad? I can never tell. Ant capitalism confuses the situation even further than it has done in the past – of course it always can do.

Celtic loads off barrels in pass, or tow to carry in marriage vows. In situations of extra special variety – tarry on the road right now, feeling good for nothing lasts, except true knowledge past word power – hour after hour.

And sow the seeds of conversation, rearrange the change creation. Veer right, one piece at a time – design the landscape of expressionlessness all on your own. Arrive in the moment and discover spoken vowel sounds – in and around sincere and well bred seasons reasoning requests, roam.

Real results bless our home – less of more and more is leading their hands ashore. Elements of fire down, sooth sounds around – regular recognition became framed of a friend's bereavement before the great wars of the last century. Formulas, secret recipes collect their massive emulations – echoes of past lives bliss, in ecstasies throng are the masses. For now the world is at peace – every moment counts, all at rest and feeling fine.

Representational concern and emotional resistance burns fuel for the empires return – traitors capture the moment, making history eventually ironic and thoroughly enraptured in times political endeavours. The very hand of fate breaks the ice again, thin as it may seem to be – somewhere division's cataclysmic proportions manually drive the spear of destiny into its clefted hiding place. Strangle hold on mother nature's private estate, as she grieves placidly over deep ravenous creatures now extinct. Courting ravens call each other out to fly about their lightened shadows – beat of the wing falls down on every loving thing in productive reasoning altogether.

Ordinarily transposed arboreal watering holes – strengthened within the confines of beat generations. Finally regenerating the futuristic urge of postnatal bliss and unilateral tribulation. Equilateral triangulation so-so dilapidated exposes triviality – space exhaust fumes re-absorbing weapons of ministry introductions carbon dating alternative realities. Profound metallurgic gastronomic excursions find high tension on the live wire mysteries destruction – explosions of convolution, discern an interest in toxicology through endomorphic consultation. Even in this age of purple dried fundamental escapism we are nevertheless surrounded by pseudo-religious fanaticism more of the same. Entire planetary encounters of inhospitable refugees begin to feel the need to remain unexplained – NASA bites into the indistinct capitalism of genuine inoculation.

Global domination from alien species brought here in some scientific way before the rise of the mammal – drift quietly into sedation as struggling nuclear nations blow us all away to hell or kingdom come. Focus on realities laboratorial exploration, first things first – so much for the same ol – same ol pal. Distinct patterns of interracial terrestrial lifeforms integrate into modern civilisations functioning bodies of free flowing physicality. Spiritually adept beyond our understanding – today, here and now, before you lies another realm of possibilities to extend the frontiers of our magnificent creation; Earth.

Mother of elements, ancient heritage, culture and tradition – references and bibliographies to get the message across through censorship and astonishing absence of intelligence or common reference to humanities denial of imaginative conviction – for dismissal.

Explanation resembles similar changes from creatures of psychologically challenging psychosis – in other words regular ordinary human beings. Deep meaningful disintegration of thousands of years of developmental scientific discoveries – nothing personal, just shrewd fragments of experienced opinion.

Subsequent deliveries of substance have rendered even me speechless to a degree – inoculation then seemed to be the intelligent thing to develop for the average mind. Resembling creatures of dreamlike apparition and subconscious representations otherwise unknown to healthy wholesome mentally prepared frontiersmen such as I.

Ready for the onslaught of aggressor and physical layabouts of non-existent intellect or thought provoking theories – warriors for forgotten causes, fighting from enslaving slave mentalities. Soaked in potions of otherworldly daemons craving to breath the air in which we soak the energy's we share together daily. Fragments of their former selves ripped gently from bone and tendons treasury – nothing compared to what's arriving on our worldly doorstep soon.

Rattle cages of ridicule; shake violently the bars that bind the saintly madness of our minds. Then preaching the silence in assurance of the whole – mould breaking liquid oozing through a hole in the wall.

Found greater challenges further out from oceans reach, twisted balls of mercury float high above the shores of egocentric magnetism. Attention to detail finds nothing further from the truth – overall distinctive distances remotely assemble successive admissions indiscriminately. Before the end is nigh behaviour breakdowns to the undertow – international operation inexplicably swings to the right side of the road. Suggestions all in this continued disturbance of tranquilities memory outbreak abductee of reason, logic and struggle in their suffering.

Postnatal depression mysteriously presides above the rest of all surgical mutilations – quickly releasing memory to the mix. Rounding off special favours with noxious anxiety and with overwhelming might of wisdoms meteorite.

Beguiling metamorphosis of requiem mass exodus consortium – method to the masses madness of journeys near completion to an end. Of additional sacrimonious encounters, trial ovulations combined experimental profanity, covers the former frontiers in all ways but one, general expectation. Unilateral expectation falls well before the end – indiscriminate behaviour takes the heavy fall towards freedom's next adventure. Love in all things love of all things, brags continuously of astonished enlightened beings in fear of their lives. Once again a fearless whisper smash and grabs its way through the boredom of experienced men and women, arching its back along the timelessness of duality. Dreams come true – full of strange delight and incredible moments of drownings silent gifts to the dying shamanic soon to be born again once where warriors mountain people. Credible sorcerer in crowning glory breaking laws that don't exist – stretching across tidal waves of self loathing and horrific psychological crimes that turn this wide world to slime.

Disorder and suffering become you well; too soon, the sound of moaning oozes from the depths of savage hell-shadows reach out from every corner, for your shoulders shelf-life is on their wicked wilting menu. On the inside once again a fool cries for help in every way they can – beyond the grave then, a place of recognition for all mankind, blind, deaf or dumb to truth, through painful, bitter end. Gifted witness will observe then their own credibility before ascension to the executive position to which they well deserve this treat – indeed; furious anger awaits the blundering idiot that is born of shame. So the final chapter of the buffoon is played out on the head of the vile creature that is worm.

Purpose finds vexation with such things as have no name – for all the world to see in glory fortunately love and hate have much in common. Physical evidence breaks even eventually – soaked in significance, glowing with a magnetism unsurpassed in vegetative subterranean ridicule of distinct global clarification. Characters disintegration, overexposed to infraradiated carbonisation detox therapy cloned the entire area completely, one step at a time. Disappear into the abyss, unearthing complex puzzles themselves far beyond the understanding of most consolidated hip-shot theorists of our day – immediate in reply and inundated with unexpectant cyber-punk malevolent factors organisation.

Always in complete categories for whatever occasion arises – opportunity knocks out their lights again, metaphorically speaking like a hitchhiker on moonshine. Read between the lines of any normal astrological cluster – red-hot survival in sacred orbits decline. Finesse stretches out infinitely – what is the sky? Stars.

Stopped our favourite on the street for a moment of magic in this dreary city swell – spell-enchanted dreams singing freely in cool breeze. Gales froth up for seashell mermaids drunk on joy and hope swells up inside like a journey of opium dreams helter-skelter mid summer insanity. Joined at the hip in freedom screaming oust the beggar free the slave, fill this empty vessel seriously. Face in testimony rewards the innocent incandescence of pure idolatry – slow and clear the birth of jade and mysterious destinies, embroidered faiths labyrinths nice n' easy each and every last time and time again, just for your entertainment everyone and all encounters let them be, for crying out loud live and let live, endless infinity of trembling hearts at my command for the very first time. Genuine survivor, winks at clusters of heavenly bodies behold the tabernacle of God say he that has a dream – salaam malekam Moslem man – look to women for wisdom. Babylon is come to ruin twice – vehicles assigned to humidity, strategised for hybrids in captivity – alarm thy neighbours to the truth of rehabilitation. Capitalise formation realistically conscientious and geographical compositions abound – before the fact we are scheduled for infections resurrection. Towards a higher goal I fold my bones before the cold wind blowing steadily down the silent passage of mourning instabilities.

Desperate for self same endgame incommunication systems of denial or reflexing cotton bud vanities cordial – empty heads participate in our exclusive comedy. Error of the propeller minded activist in tune with all coincidence and probabilities latest illustration. Some of us actually believe the implications of outrageous acts, extradinarily enough as it may sound – with hearts of gold so we have found it quintessentially profound to a degree. Scheduled cancellations drive the venge fuelled tragedy forwards – vilified beyond their graves, into the after life's concave vision of apostasies revenge. Remarkable recoveries after years of divine interventions –

transcendental experimentation assassinates the opposition's return. Heavens above I am inclined to implicate in equal measure for higher learning – towering along the nightingale's perfection as in lover's frequent reinvention.

Solid as coronation, driven by desire, fired up fascination, fuelled fires of gravely emancipation – diversified in honourable discharge. Obvious personality dyslexia permeates the globe in honour of captive audiences non-existent acquaintances – blockbusters organisation spurs the moment on forever. Burial place of intellectual reservation rendezvous with honourable quotation – tombstones break existence from their epitaph's engraving. Company is still of artistic peregrinations about the sound searching out and about for a soul here in battle worn worm hole called Dublin.

Miniscule redemption scratches through the sky, fleeting confirmation of the uneasy friendliness of desperations tragic desecration. Obligatory defiance leaves the globe of sacred apprehension blind – conformity destroys the atmosphere for jealous tribulation. Winding stairwell search for less is more than any mind can make a mess as well the sinking feeling dwells – endearing return of evenings mysterious adventure. Concentrated in this discursive surmise has talented invention scratched the surface – our surprise is welcome.

Then to reinvent one self as intensely and contemporarily complicated as possible in time fascinates the whole pursuit of pleasures impact with value and supreme repose. Insomnia pops its endless head up again without a doubt of fascination or supreme theosophy exposed. Anxiety debates hallucogenic delirium instead of inexperienced nostalgia without reason – treated with the utmost discretion deliberately. The first of its kind, a universal river of expression finds the times we live in unbearable and inexcusable for all intents and purposes. An everlasting empire of recognition far more frightening than ever before, translates probable inconsistencies throughout our condition. Rudimentary fascination perfects anticipated literary anxiety complete in technique and with an exhibition of remote possibilities.

Seek and yee shall find manuscripts of ancient esoteric pursuits never before uncovered since so hastily disguised in exclamation or retreat – driven to distraction, charged exactly to a tee. Often ignored unfortunately – speakeasy suave sophisticated and adorned in goddess religion.

Its all metaphysical compromise, launched randomly at our viscal visitation – clans encounter offensive is then ill repressed, beyond conversion; hospitalised. Disclosures treasury swell extracts the mortal membranes of our lives in converted conversation, deepens to dementia or insane personalities – surprise is far from our association. Through investigations into uncharted foreign waters uncover their mistakes, blindly erratic sensation keeps hope alive.

Organised exhibitionism calls patronisingly across indignations supper of the last and first abiding kind – gesture in a state of indigestion are we not comforted in caricatures disquiet – forgive me if I'm wrong capitulation.

Begrudger's ill equation, hypothesis or understanding of the same – the exception that still improves that thick-skinned rule Confucius says, all men are equal in state and style. Indifferent influence kindly finds the time to practice absolutely that power of disobedience that all are subjected upon – singularly, one at a time. Divided in action, common in ideological persuasion – ideally magnified for limitations distinction. Crying out enough rivalry for the time being – advocating a deep chronological experience never before performed for illegal audiences around this Earth of ours.

Objective desecration personifies engaging objectivity with obvious meanings of loutish evolutionary discrepancies – embraced loyal biographies of protracted multiplicity precise in every way. Liturgies misbegotten post-mortem dries thin the ice between the distances divide – in exchange for intrigue and external misinformation. Grasped only just by chance of a cosmopolitan adventures fragmentary enterprise – extreme caution is advised if we are to suggest otherwise. Multilingual reluctance of translation leaves the metaphysical behind – macaronic musicianship drives us further on to our ambition. Recriminations quintessential heartstring, faithlessly strives on for a change in circumstance without great difficulty of recognition for a supreme being of this sort. Languages oppressive collections estranged legacy resides in a compromised position - dispossessed contributors arrange themselves in seriously uncomforting angles above the below. Bird of prey arguably referred to as the torment of skies inhabitance – do you choose the mercenaries dream of vengeance. Invasion of the white mans dream, messengers flying high through the fog of foundation screaming victim, victim, victim you will remain so and stay the same old same 'ol. Striptease *feng-shui* arguably arrested in this philosophical oversimplification, magnifies topography with national tribulation and surprise – redeemed wise owl manoeuvring swiftly on.

Towards a higher goal, rootless information unsurpassed qualifications rectified through similar pursuits in global swarms illusion stratosphere philanthropist elation. Born again for a futuristic vision of excellence never before seen or will ever uncovered dream be over streams of evolution then. A sociopathic nightmare, increases narrative offerings to a stretcher bearers ill-equipped participation – for all mighty invitations are inevitable yet financially fortuitous, this generation plays quizzically, the frivolous game. For no hand that has personal perception gains from a momentary lapse of sanity – ramifications viewpoint struggles on to measure arms distance; swift and sure.

Unsavoury cannibalism calls unorthodox techniques to charge after the anthropological androgenic syndrome is released beyond repair to tax their mannerism. Indefinitely unsavory despair appears exhaustive for inhibitive reporters of the sun dried kind – wish well companions censorship is high and dry indefinitely. Beauty streaks across vivid depictions of the evolutionary landscape divided by the troubled mind – emphasising pleasures informal heritage. Domination of tense dramatic interplay, opens doors for structural demonisation – multiple storyboards dominion experiences grievous bodily harm. For reasons otherwise unbeknown to all examples of explorer's trepidation, here we have it, a formal display on abstinence, sequence and a capacity for something very different from the norm. Extreme disfigurement immobilises contemplative procedures capability inescapable and unforgiving entertainments of impulse and dramatic persuasion leave mysterious vibrations far behind.

Chapter Five

All new possibilities prevent tragedy for health and happiness and are ultimately divine enclosures of stressed propulsions solutions. Dreadful dread softens all systems indefinitely moral dilemma, survives temporarily sanitised. Moving forwards and figuratively speaking-tasks beyond nihilistic formula, for a forged compromise. Blatantly immersed in realism so speak out to find like minds thinking generously of each other's failure. Celebration of our loss and extreme prejudice becomes lethargic and just plain horrible-together affirmation takes all of the blame continuously. Denial, denial, denial, excitement still avails life's relationship for destruction in retail trademark centaur bereavement, packaged goods department.

Mortal combat breathes easy contentment and is ordained more importantly for instruction rather than stupidity incarnate. The real you, is without barriers – be open, be empty and full to the brim of ministries declaration. Time to win, time to lose – transindentally transfixed conspicuous success with personal impresario in tow. Come hell or high water, there's going to be hell to pay – the likeness of inspiration following in form. The intermission braces inclusively towards himself. God Almighty – an improbable frequency is declared.

The standing ovation is remarkably scheduled through thick and through thin as keen as mustard is fever pitch, never proportioned. Between the drag of normal working days, I think not of mortalities events.

To speak eagerly of swift justice personified and for wherever the focus should be. Satisfaction guaranteed, for now, famous portioned and the all-important in set-up is grandly reduced and originally insane. Disgraced Heroin-chic, some Australians are born again, Christians rhetoric.

The benefits of restaging share in the quick-check regulations electrical shock-therapy conditions in abnormal chase. Seeking liberty, starting with lingo on the offering rails – a hardened warrior all the way to the finish line. Self same quickens up on the difference – much more smaller than the big time comes. Best of luck on the witches march auld fella – see you soon Lingo – Jingo.

Go! Jump it well our bell hopping seeker – followed over by extra, to loop the charmers off colour, flow grows quickly on down to slope behind lucky swindley lengths further back out on the race; the hare is always the one to catch. Second from the left she crashes hard about two or three behind the double – that's for combinations error.

France landed first along the bottom - just diseased and their novice is winners well too-do. The good day from first to last is inconvenienced still – this fine filly surely hurled abuse – very dark and small the back. To respond in elaborate disappointment, firm and quick and set up for tomorrow. Building serious pokus from the grove of Ladbrokes, features over three miles on the lucky gamble – with all the others. Time is meaningless – therefore no decision is definitely on the cards followed by another onslaught of insult we are but features, caught in the middle again. Strange fruit hangs far too far above my head – missiles of defeat full again of innocent blood fall, our souls empire infinitely lengthens; strengthens somebody else's body mind soul and spirit for friendship never ever ends. Mirror image, and of some other place – messenger of Mars, reach out forever forwards, out of time in need – our heads, are outdone.

Some simple pretence breaks down the secret barriers of understanding – lose my head on the flaming edge, is it any wonder! Some of us are and more so, some not, even truly here and now. Perfect portal in face- mind's eye for some everlasting love. Don't let it show – just let it go. Seven sacred seas joined at the hip, together in an instant. Shaking shock of careful manipulation here we have it. Moronic ignorance and evil, forever banished from Earth shall be – thrown out of mirror's wide window in deep intrepid isolation and solitarily confined. Drip-dried on druidic dusty universal highways-stretched far and mighty wide between galaxies some billions of light-years away and only a second's breath between us.

Far to divide greatly the diseased from the healthy and leave well enough alone. Amused internally and abused so much beyond measure for elongated periods of time. Each and every step a little easier than the last – some new terminal insult to endure, some ignorant effort at communication just to please me. Into the idle orphanage of selling the soul sitting menstruation cycle catechism for all our unhappy people – How to ruin other's in three easy steps.

First let yourself go, the power will take over, well in fact it already has – let us do the rest. Mystery some say hardens such suffering, for divine life is a calling.

Then trust what I say, palaces made of gold are always painted ivory – permanent manicure of dreams. Criss-crossed many waters of the long cold winter land is before you. Leap into this well of silence. Tell me everything is true-speak of the cosmos ever so earnestly – whatever is on offer, comes my way, fearless fears of change, fears of truth, fears of eternal youth and joy and simple innocence. These infamous sins of your forefathers have landed on all but our doorstep. Death follows with them – fierce and deadly eyes drawn deep into cold hard sockets of night torment, pain and misery, our own demise. Poet prophet far from rest and respite, can you see now the futile effort, sin and infidelity bring to simple minds?

This mob of ours is so far gone now – beyond recall most of them still brokendown and bewildered. Far out wisdom, without the effort of knowledge is forsaken – humane hope springs eternal yet lies just out of reach. Secret suicide note left in hand – morbidly denied moreover such romance leaves a tear in the eye. Slipping ever so gently onwards – a hard road of old cold stone psychological and physical cruelty in accessible climatic and unfit conditions is waiting. Bones broken and flesh torn open – blood pours painfully from my veins onto this dirty rugged terrain. Soulless emotionless men's – horrid strangled desperation fluid of monstrous invention. Here and now Satan's army recruits infinitely to torment those of us that again have fallen from ourselves. Ourselves look around – holes in the ground, contemplate the tyranny of dust and desolation. Rats and rabbits spill their guts out on the pavement of our lives – destroyed are my fallen people – fallen from grace. The molested now are patented and purified in darkness and simplicity, shines forth.

O please! Can I spell it out for you – learn to foresee that horror of race that is more than men. This alien race, alien culture cannot know what lies awaiting in our DNA. Creatures of ill intent – inhumane objects of desire – hedonists burnt at the funeral pyre lie in wait to descend on the children.

Inbred nations of Earth, the beast has won over the battle, now we have lost him the war. Alright, on a lighter note, it gets worse before it gets any easier. What? Did you think a little meditation and some minor miracles could cure you! Take a good look at the critics eye's – taste their hatred and ingest their scorn, it will fuel your work far into the future my brother. Enter the tomb of all that is your career – all will be revealed those that suffer youth and seek the truth. But it's not a pretty sight *mon-ami*; it's grotesque beyond belief. A new man-made reality and its yours for the taking.

Oust this scum filled galaxy for all its worth and I will love you, held together by a storm below zero 0 venom of spider sunk resentfully beneath your skin. Human rights declaration so richly deserves attention indeed – forthwith indefinitely. Determination rules, supreme cordials reckless have we been, moments of magic night – gig madness in effect, is not our peaceful providence overcome? In dire circumstance forsooth, the crisis deepens through positions of administration and total annihilation in effect immediate and complete.

Adverse features follow shortly the order of the day in essence of peaceful solution. Delicious and dead lives enter a new land of graves and partition – the lower levels of hell rub, together unilaterally. Equivalent production hits an all-time high – envy oozes out of the woodwork, drastically and desperate for some attention of some dimensional structure or other. Poised for battles ready for war, constant and exclusively denied in the mourning time of your soul. Depending on the multicoloured inequalities of starvations rebates in disposal and congregation charities comprehensive guide to the galaxy of your choice. A new law is in order indeed – involving immediate action and great sacrifices.

Some involuntary action deems to contempt the void vocal opinions the ordinary locals visions of a better future within ourselves. Challenged by the facts that demolition has destroyed our lives, is far enough by the other side – them that are driven forwards by the need for greed. Their starvation of the inner self brings with it desolation and blind ignorance – to say nothing of rightful ways. Wrathfully exclusive depths of invitation to readily dredge our tradition as if diseased and deformed in manner. Trial by error, loop the loop – hang them high, break their bloody backs on barbed wire love. Time to payout for the ferryman, we have crossed over to the other side. Now that some of us learn to leave well enough alone, the impartial others are lost, cast aside as if by accident only. The horned-god of old in simple disguise, has shed a mournful tear from, his eye and laid the Earth to waste. Quickly, a combination of disease deepens gloriously on our heads, as if by power be denied.

All this results intoxication of the same prehistoric résumé Lucifer whose name I may not say. A rush towards resolution and peaceful solution, sure to coincide directly in combination or hostage situation. Imagination takes aim with doggedness and determination – advancing tirelessly out towards the broken goal. So far, so good, in agreement of the same insurmountable goal suspension bridge of inevitable justification and disrepair global clarity. Institutions of souls deforestation – the worm slithers his way into and the wholesomeness of body incarnate. Jealous rage anxiety becomes the nemesis of today, as is every day. How can you live your life this way? I hear you say. It's easy when you know, how say I.

Eyes closed shut, propped equally exhausted and precariously put out on troubled waters may I remark. The bride looks remarkably unscathed by the dramatic outcome of events – turntables that this way inclined, visualising a quick recovery. A desperate hesitation forces equal victory once again – a greatly disputed fact among the forces. Doubt sets in; the doubt of guilty men always seems to sail on full tide mystery event of solitude places great mistake by lion's mane. Currents drag on simple mind of the goats get ready to fight around your ground, the heathen is everywhere, love is lost, hitherto seek sanctuary in Satan's grotto – know whom you faithlessly serve man – because we that wish to be free, then serve righteously the master of divine power.

Stay then oh sacred macrocosm of blazing passion, hold still to your intrepid dreams. Strive ever onwards to a higher plain – stay the course of fluctuation, the day's adventures. Humble passengers indeed, find ways of misdemeanour to endure the rigours in course with cure on armed fortune. Rest and to feature what you are, a poet or companion – heave-ho the tall eternal glory of youth day; yonder goes the whirlwind of times idle ways, to our voyager; flames of torment linger on, their intrepid lessons learnt, but not yet message be. Its an incendiary search and destroy mission, flex your muscles – seen to be believed forever and a day insider sanitised ill equilibrium – reflex mortal spoils diluted solution and to a tee. Blink and you'll miss it matey our muck savage simpleton dork supreme mountain magic maestro – queen of the softly spoke ministry of colossal strength equality in crème de la crème society incarnate. All global frustration brings bounties of strange celebration to our door once again. Poor mouth gremlins crock out the park of madness – real places, real people have we been made into machines already, or always awaiting to be sent down by Love's Divine powers.

Exact and to the mark of infinite possibilities we're inclined to imagine Morpheous might indeed, agree to public humiliation and disembowelment. Brooding on the bards recent revival in jest; complex matters are at hand, brute and barren land have I seen purged of institution and incendiary (i.e.?) devices, of which bled the humans body dry in much more than is blood. Torture chamber, is colonial karma gone ape-shit altogether? Took a look, it's further to the future, see the fleeting history of our pastlife too frail and useless. Brave our brothers; we no longer seem to care. Much more to the point it's easily done to say in no roundabout way at all as if our amazement be, tried and satisfied, content to be at ease so easily. In no possible and in exact way, ill at ease and out with intoxicatingly stupefied repugnant devils and necromancers of far, far lower level ignorance altogether. Locked my minute self away from mortal danger into an open ocean of love and harmonious well-being. Dive I head first through bliss-filled avenues of hope and divine power. Instrumental again in the recovery of thousands before and many after in this portal of new discovery.

Absorbing only positive emotion is mostly more of an art than an illusion of the schizophrenic and paranoid mind. Content to be beside ourselves, again within a closer environment to home. Safe are we in crowds together and powerful in war. Church mice holding clowns at bay, safely rejected is the joker – forever is indeed such a long and lonely time. It seems to suit some of us, some of us are deaf, dumb and blind indeed to glorious fate – disaster strikes a wild unbroken twisted path to mountain paths above. An altar of sapphire is built and there remains until this day a strength of strange delight. Roads through all their inherently ancient woods cut by the hardest steel and chains, drawn into the light of mighty mystic shores. Here we go again brothers, mothers, fathers and all the others smelting all the way – sister of the dawn, daughter of eastern dance and wild winter morning rise! The sun again has come to skies bright with rain. We work on, walk tall and breath well the intestinal pain of life – seek and yee shall find the best way is always the simplest, blessed raging road of starlight tread, winding twisting stream crossed path of ours in mind.

A leisurely stroll among the popular thief's – live life a long way with many men's dreams. Far too late is our tribe's trial and test – always good to wait till it's at best on the turn and tide, slip, swell high. Treasure takes us home today, over this way all is said and sundry. Leave it up to me my friends, take your places now and then – whisper words of wisdom please, take it easy and strive on swiftly. Broken, harmful hunting with knives, drift away upon the ice – lift our heads high if you're able, spill the milk upon the table. Finish off with the slime like forms, open to our rich embrace – empty of mysterious animation and searching for some advantageous results. Put an end to doubt, for once and for all – terminate falseness and superiority forever. Bring to a close completely – the end is nigh mentality. Drawn to our conclusion the pretence of wisdom and knowledge – instead increase the flow of time and time again, efficiency to the last drop. Friendship rules this place divine – it lasts a long long time.

All in accordance with, the law of the book – take time to totally bare all elements to the wind. With renewed endeavour, comply with all standards – in close contact with some phenomenon or other, in tow, continuously. Far from home in separation, singing always of the joy of desire's temptress, in tone and present company, expecting local adversaries. Petrified purpose dealt with and definitely with strength, forever more from a simple mind childhood. Your heart should immeasurably beat out of proportion completely – ah! There you have it my favourite, there you have it now. For it's sure to be impressed you are by the immeasurably great, and glorious past, present and future dates on the calendar that are awaiting yee on far costal reaches chill out zone.

Maybe it's because, because because you know – the one thing in my life says you, that calms me down mack. Search for the spoken words that sweetly vanished the mark, so obviously is mistaken – a delightful calling of trembling hermaphroditic hands so cleverly concealed.

Our misbegotten marksmen finally force the mark into a functioning yet far-fetched idea, royal junk ship, voyeuristic flotilla. Specific slander more friends and their might – brings home the mess of supernova. Again and again we try and try – forever and a day, whatever you blatantly might say. Break for the border amigo – chase away the soul of indigo, pure and unrefined. To dream the night away – don't give up on that rebound, for I have found another champion for the blues this evening. Our very own brother good man – here he is, on the warpath ready for more, how I adore the very thought of you. Make the most of it, ready, steady, go – it's all yours, take it away bro. Get out the door, down the street Mexico's only a walk away, we're gonna make it yes we are, yes, all the way, top o' the wicked world ma – yee'ha! Once and again.

Chapter Six

Torment and begrudery, witness a dysfunctional universal urge to destroy all that lies before us – longing for the end of torment and oblivion. Look towards the future is now my friend, 'till the will is come and gone from your soul forevermore – turn your back on all traitors and fellow evilmen and then your will is done. A fix of some incredible high profile impartial access all areas concoction squares us all the way through – indescribable pain finds its way out of this mess and into a more sophisticated drug induced stress-free existence. For instance the mere presence of any organic provisions expels any illusion there may have been intoxication of any kind – installation speaks of disorder; disease enters the mind. Find a fixation possibly proven technical misadventure of the chemical kind, strewn across their imaginary explanations of this tiny little world they desperately cling to like rats on Chinese glue paper. Spoken of comforts great and blindingly discredited to any nation north and south of the equations unsurpassed democracy of the here and now promotionary engagements sociopathic devolution of this normal freemantle clearance sale of the century over the counter omnipotent clairaudient experimental interview. Such is the same kind of cutting edge instalments that we are so conditionally used to over here in the hemisphere of hopelessness – it certainly ain't easy being green boyo, no not at all. There you have it, plagiarism at its best, better that the real thing baby, a natural phenomenon of primordial evolution that is exposed to the earths intestinal absinth of harmonious hell for leather painfree do as I please animal activity. For the more malevolent microcosmic mentalities, relief springs eternal in the form of the most toxic form of antifreeze ever to exit the bag and enter the brain, then drain your life away drop by precious, perilous drop – to remain at all times at a safe distance for safeties sake, agreed for futures profit and yet remain connected to the phospherent flow of greedy little men, insane remedies mysterious connection to the mind. Some morbid delusion that's secretly evaporates before the eyes in silent admission then leaves us blind – torrid river rages back and forth, the flowing tide remains the same. An even sinister revolution, sings songs of praise for dissolved in our prime, leaves well enough alone the dark interior – finished Mexican pride as spins on a tired old git.

Sometimes the light shines through strong and powerful as ever it may be, this day or that, for whatever reason it can be – times have moved on friendly or not, the pain in raids of bushmen lingers on; the sound of the dead. Sovern trial or sorcerers judgement, governs aftermaths exclusion –

deep in the bowels of oblivion lies descent and glad to be rid of it am I, to be sure indeed, muck savage! Reverence descends on our esoteric exclusion, from ear to ear am I, in danger of conclusive interference; leaves a lot to be desired, our amplifications demise.

Where the hell have I been? Why did I go there – How long have we ignored the fact that we're living in denial, you and I, ourselves that is. Inconvenienced to the last drop of impure particles of opposing destinations supreme delusionary contradiction of inflammatory discharge and in hereditary affirmation impresario, sublime expressionism is redeemed. Only temporarily of course, since this is the time of remorse filled dreams of incredible gravitational decay and exploitation, generated democratically for future generations electrical desecration and immoral interplay. Distance yourself from this universal skulduggery for an instant of self relocation and find intense pain – leisure incarnated and active continuation in extreme measure of present company discarnate implosion. Representation of all recognised pharmaceutical produce gives precedence to the credence of imbecilic bodies silent procession through the dark night of the soul. Ra, god of the sun is with us in our time of need, reminding us that most of this modern civilisation is incomplete, unnecessary meaningless garbage – useless in every way, full of the horrors and inconsistencies and ready for the end. Oh modern meaningless mess, defrosting certain death each and every step of the way – shoved in their face impossibly compensated abnormalities, arboreal standardisation. Overcome thousands of immovable objects of indomitable ferocity one by one, equal in measure and elasticity. Direct compatibility for everything ever living or in decisive and outstanding decoration, made to order, inevitably inarticulate misjudgements melancholic and tender in order and procedure. Against animal testing for any reason whatsoever relating to the larger issues at hand for a modes function-disinterest freaks more violently towards the left side of the road, more to mention. Blank stares searching out of windows, moaning fervently of better times ahead – search and destroy merchandisers; bleak winters ahead. Summers come and going gone my son, the truth is rarely said – some springtime when all is remembered, we will be forgotten sure enough.

Furious shortcomings truncheon heartless meanderings open minds of sickly foreign devils – smuggling jesters blind escapism without the need for sound bites. Driven by a desire for hazardous overpopulation and subsequent disruptive behaviour developed by a complete lack of interest in anything remotely connected with Hyde, the potion crazed alter ego of Jekell, doctor of generally every ailment known to mankind. In particular the condition formerly known as mad in the head for the benefit of those listening here tonight. Benign cancerous growth I think the word is called, fully functioning moronic stupidity, reeling of contagious idiocy – abandonment of any capable intellect of any kind, fundamentally flawed I think therefore I am irreversibly sad, mentally, physically and soul-spirit is willing but the flesh is weak kinda juvenilely done over. Unavailable for any normal kind of communication of any sort at any time day and night – demonically possessed in everyway known to man. These are my companions - through this journey called life – inadequate audiences without ascension to innovativety – through day or night, a fruitless projection of disquiet from each bizarrely unimaginative person or red devil, as the case may be. Evocative disrepair taking further on the horizontally perpendicular treasures at any fragile dysfunction of momentary fracture, rendered together instead of combined force virility man over candle burns on your part time heartache transparency. One for one and all out luminosity compared to insulation stations substitute migraine for the masses founder puritans unorthodox deities creation, domesticity eradication functioning abdominal gasses – stressed out mass exodus, production overnight satisfactions guaranteed prearranged recommendation. Recreation of essential oil oblivion activities in denial all the while for free productive thirty three never sees stimulation elevated – corridors of toxic annihilation and all things hereditary: overused werewolves are very much the vagabond, theories for trickery and disfigurement by the while unsuccessfully moralising and deflamatory. Ridiculed conflicting shadows of emotion and elusive disgrace leaves us blind – charged through hills in our dream worlds demolition. Swarming illustrations heart filled escape through the hidden valleys of mysticism to stand beyond the warm glow of sacred spiritual treasure, then join together hands of joy and peace – breathing fresh air where I feel free. Haven't you heard of accidental journeys stolen against the grain of time, bending fate and stretching your mind beyond its limited frontier – visit another place, space out for a while, don't you want to? I do. Redeemed in fortune and past life forensic release for an instant of bliss and electric vibes pilgrimage. Disfigurement is gospel here in extreme solidarities temporary hide away and memories of our multiple rhythmic sensations are common, in cold consideration before the fact of evolutions elite fanaticism. Going underground slowly but surely with a multitudinal fascination for revival of the finest historical nature we require – finesse, durability and perfection for all out war.

Distance yourself from all moderation, satisfy yourself according to fancy and whim, dedicate yourself to ineffective substitution of all things great and useful. Force the end to shorten its allotted deadline and swoop upon the painful busyness of necessary evil – fall from grace one last time, how about it, the moon is rising steadily. On the market for a supply or imprecise majority rules okay deterrent for originality – there's always a price to pay. The ferryman is bored with life and feels just barely delighted with himself, again try as we may, she fails in preparation as his wife bears fruit well and true for soothing regularity, is due and none too soon. So-called regularity scrapes across the floor; of Jung's incompetence at capturing the golden orbs of joy, we expose then truth and false interrogation, slowly but surely and with great trepidation.   I supply devalued ministries future generations anonymity for astonished gentle creatures precise unachievements ill evasion – radical change in unrequited cosmic challenges, love, when furnace fuel ravages this costly creature comfort, vague removal from the force results in subtle constitution. Absent minded reason fails to see the point; inside shaman's powerful will does sick intestine chill the bone of common sense, each season and to the quick, pedantic stillness weave some magic still for poison caused the spill to stick in some small weakness end of days, is raised heads to the ground for all of us to see. Of all the pressure on this sound cannot we all agree, to leave unjust desecration to the past. Will never let us better spot the level of artistic phials, full of blood inside or ill at ease we ill remain to sully vixens measure still, stains the walk of inhuman forgotten risk-talk to me my heart is willed for beating, starts again, the passion plays on and on.

Over to the beaten generations name, are we ill equipped, flamed up and shameless, for gestations vegetation shifts the blame on mixed emotion. Doubles up on wasted leisure, redirects this liberation more than ever before, something's stirring by my bedside – cool breeze burns cold in the chamber below my head. Thump on the floor to my left, then closer again and shivers run through me, first slowly then malevolent and threateningly abhorrent apparitions – over exposed transition phase of existence moves towards the light yet fears the hammer fall of justice for a life of sinful ignorance. More movement reaches back and calls out from the distance 'help me' for the good cause calls out – peace be with you brothers and so to be accepted to oracle own teen Wicca whatever you may want, roam outside the thunder clones. Lightening fast and sunshine silver, finish hell-bent murder river – touches tone bleak a weary river flows north towards the heathen shore. Fallen angels chance a ride to ease the wall of stone that skies crown golden edge shines glistening, futuristic vibes, ride on the tail of truth and justice ride. Damned ones enter doomlined caves and fail to curse the demon slaves – fall far into the ocean brother, fall far beyond broken body and twisted hands of destiny, strive for lethal revenge. Empty guts wide open on the curve, this way and that when all else fails – seething destruction never fails to please in furnace fire or oven. Coveted snail space strangles inquisitions far out shores of hate, a decision making man of woman. Essential compounds open vessel stimulates thin devils grinning widely, outcast and concubine – cringing stories told well before the great beheading of oriental moneyman's addition to the western worlds sedation. Essential vicissitudes break the face of reason, strength in numbers, instant seasons to your door – Finish all the points of vision, speak to me of eastern lights. Then all of life shall walk away from sick and dreary mental illness – barriers break down, far away from hunger, give the chance of change a try, its useful if your wise.

Charming underdogs eternal charity speaks through tongues of lard – how hard could it be, to dive angelically into a new order of symmetry and perfection. Even as I speak of clear resentful creatures, all is love in sceptres cheery call – eventually flames clear out towards a more carefree existence of originality and elegant natural phenomenon. Dominion over famous creatures mediumship drives out fortune and incompatible relationships linked more and more with strenuous progression of strict duality in evidence of final plans to intercept. For an easier time of it, higher percentages hold small evidence of prophecy and reincarnation – there is a paranormal world in existence. Although in another context completely to our normal experience of real-worldliness that is not attributed to 'antilife' forces such as adharmic activity or drug intake. As per usual strange occurrences only happen post-trauma or near death misadventure, such is making the best of a bad situation. Fascination with premonition and psychic experimentation calls for abuse of mind, body and soul in the laypersons everyday use – introduced by drop jaws the world over. I am still surrounded by monkeymen and psychic maniacs left over from the devils soul supper, apocalypse and Armageddon warming up for the kill, slowly but surely is all inclusive perishable mentor madness incurable.

Distance from stringy vegetation and apoplexy determination leaves us homeless as far as homelessness disappears, through major strife, appears dyslexic – storming writings automation doors the lore invasion; sense? Making academic sense so many times and I don't need your lies, you're a million miles away. Invaluable supernatural editorial fools decrease in their natural provisions – I lie down with the dogs and rise with the fleas. Fixture fear no more the liaison of freedoms eternal war on want – use the power of system in your system. Call clear for definitions dreamlike clarity and close your heart, at all times, never let it go. Unison – alive and real, really inventions form, breaks the frame of verse – 'till pain gives way. Curving curses fold on stretching vocal incendiaries for a slice of life – for what must have been a never ending torment and struggle, slithering close on useless skinflint spirit chasers. Dormant philosophical positions instruct vampiric self absorbment to decay – almost incurable due to an illness no neurosurgeon should have to deal with in anyway whatsoever.

Seek and ye will find different explanations for mental illness and disorder of the human condition – communal imperialism, Chinese colonial superiority in temple torn Tibet. We want horrific destruction of Zen! Me have no peace, me sick – you sick! You sick coz you no handle sick in head Chinese oriental communist scuzball! You racist! Etc, etc – situation do or die. Bitter inbreeding is no fault of mine I say; you my personal apocalypse, foreign devil dishevelled. I and I is national psychosis, driven to distraction over mutual attraction to disease and self bathing – controlling disillusion over materialisation of common causes for psycho psychotic disorder, a terminally vexing ailment orientals have developed into an art form. Forgive me Chairman Mao; don't get me wrong, love your enemies, always, even though they are our own personal dog from hell. Interconnected, love and hate through inarticulate frenzied assault on the senses – then romance rounded the corner in the guise of wolverine oriental goddess, all is forgiven, all is forgiven. How does thy wholesomeness wake in those sweet cheeks of yours.

Overkill takes all the thrill out of it, rock 'n roll large 'n livin for the good times, stars in midnight blue, how dare you be an artist here in the emerald isle. Don't you know it's all a lie to your royal blindness. Textural morality leaves us high and dry repetitively – doom is close at hand friends of Muérthé. Asked questions from my family, could their possibly be a chance that this here life is momentary madness – back to childhood when all is crystal clear, the heart is soaring through my soul, basic fundamental clarity. Voices from our past, you can't be serious bud – here is now, there is sacred joy and harmony. I wish I could explain how it seems to change, slowly but surely towards the end – simple social grace, leads the way endless evenings bloom. Share the space, winding down, summers empire greatly cease templates ancient records wisdom, covet sounds of space uneven. Sombre mood shaves treetop close, double echoes on your toast. I'll tip the balance, overdose of lucid memoirs seclusion of the surreal topography historical revolution. Peace and quiet after a mental freeway of a day – strange enough constellation beguiling and predominantly hermaphroditic encounters of the second or third exhibitive reconoitter bowl endeavour movement thingy. Irrelevant roman emperor violates the curtain call exquisitely – precise moment of military exhilaration strings out the sure enough methods of indivisibility and blatant feast upon imaginatively carnivorous priests evocation. Wonder fulfils the vacuum of our lives, one by one, elegant demographic trajectories vacate the strings of emeralds and sapphires, in doubt of unaccompanied sorcerers incantations. Unbeknown to ourselves there is requirements in tow for information from otherworldly influences such as we have yet to know. Inexplicable monstrosities overwhelming frequency on the rebound then from an overdramatic resurgence never before or seen again. In any other place on Gods green earth by woman, child or man, may there be some independent change for the foreseeable future – pleasant and pure as long as we endure this mess we are responsible for. In every impressionable way, belief or system, stars will shine forever; dust will be dust, endeavours concepts keep revolving into another reality completely. Unexplored universal technology reverses normal frequencies so as to engage the truth in very economical fashion. Oh! sweet justice sweep on the wasted years from my memory, leave insult to injury and jealous lives far behind. Same old same 'ol or so the story goes – murder in the joke box leaves misery a chance of closure, freaks the whim over dearly, still never out of time. It is a moving ministry that shakes the loom wide open, forever more along the shores of slime and dysentery, loathing foxhunt breaths full fold on tempests victims venture. Only just have we managed preliminary reports of whimsical discoveries – juxtaposition either side on the horizon. Severed hearts beating similarly just beyond the borderline of inquisition, leaving nothing to the minds headless infection, this way or that. Pleased to meet you, pleasant interruptions, do us a favour, one day at a time – break rehearsal, beginning to the end, then some. Quiet invasion of spirit guides, empty as a barstool, finished as the bride is doomed to grope nonchalant forsooth. Miraculous remembrance dishevelled flashback dreams melancholy overtones, between the fine shambolic turnaround underneath the soul of tree in favourite.

Pagan embrace leaves you blind, overtones disgraced with certain types adverse reactions to the same old grind, for whatever reason. Carrying a shovel to the graveyard with one thing on your mind – to escape the dream catchers treachery on the ledge of real reaction – fence climbing remembrance of your out of the ordinary expectations. Complete reversal outsiders course garden sultan rickshaw, when the answer is blue. Flashlight finds lean slender beams of the few, too kind for fancy whatever we do. Disappears over times, during changes in the stew – for many years to come. Water safety brings division until something's overcome, finish the mark in double time – weird soft hard sleep easy hammock shingles free the spook of inhibition. Close to the bone ghost of the past, squeaky clean overcast immediacy is dead instead of some new autopsy from the blood read skies individuality syndrome. Easier said than done go easy, something has to give so lets take it as it eases forth from one day to the next, it just fails to amuse, confused and fail to me. Indirect sensationalism justified by portacabin bliss; centuries along corroding masses historical explosions. A mouthful of new tasting maxims irrepressible continuation for torturous road things, stretch across the imagination ordinarily articulate manifestations calling for traitors quartering. Through reaching out to others in our hour of need, hatred takes a back seat, just for a moment – enter reason for final countdowns immediate speak-head clearly. Best friend is more an enemy than blood craving adversity – chain mail hold close the hand of fate, vanities betrayal. Selection can't keep up with the supergrade of this birth remembrance of the western world. Sunshine exclamation drives me crazy with reckless dedication for the muse of remorse – a short-lived succession ensures fresh revisionism. A partner in crime is equal in dedication, for along survival centuries old leaves not something to the imagination. Out doors of white magic investigative repetition thinks not of repercussion so the footsoldiers say. Attacks are stepped up mysteriously as vulnerable recommendations are accused of tenable complaints – its time to hit the hay, goodnight. Weird decisions call for cross examination of their witness without any reason at all, try and try again sacred scarification for a strong run.

Protestors gain more than all that can be gained – north moves slowly across the winds again. Acclaimed dereliction strains to be heard again, starting to beat the hard taste of yen from premium brains. Principal causes of death leading to consume the sap of our tracks are entrails – local legend has it, torture rituals dissolve our bodies indiscriminately. No second chances, promises removed, nuclear evictions openly observed – this siren keeps out figures, what a mess indeed my friends. In the future, face to face, time for a change, be still generation – before you know it, it's all over. Everybody has great reserve 'till wild animus comes out through lack of preservation a desperate quest for knowledge ends in tears and devastation. A pocket of resistance breaks the mould in new recognition skywards heading, takes hold with intrepid hesitant assistance on our behalf. Thank God someone's capable of progression and the like of report of something's or the other – tragedy losses life before parting company. Which tells us absolutely nothing at all. It's as good a theory as anything. Blatant publication of accusations for clientele, live from the studio – a practical revolutionary biotechnical program that gives a slightly different twist; that will increase the standard. Their pulling out all the stops, spreading out close contact; brings out questions for the next candidate – replacing or retracing investigative techniques. Arrested by acute mind development medication whenever a free moment arises and vacate the premises momentarily. Local shelter hospitalisation well appreciates the visual geography of these afflicted areas – the brain is a highly sensitised mechanism after all. Symphonies are created there, dreams produced and major thought provoking ideas are expelled in the blink of an eye, without a word or moment to decide on any effect. They might create dissolution; they may produce solutions, who can tell? Which one of us is to know what ingenious inspiration is composed exposed or valued – interpret it however you wish. It is time for infatuated infrastructure to get a move on – hopelessly addicted to the times we live in. Reputations left intact or just barely redeemable for remarkable recovery – it's alright to learn the facts before the fiction, so we are led to believe. So far removed from modern or should I say from everyday people who will ignore the silent subtleties that loom out before us like small diseases and deformities. The very thought itself that causes impudent effect on others can always advertise the truth but only to those that wisdom opens its doors to. In other words 'to test' is to invite the effects of cause and effect; to see the power of curiosity reversed on to the minds of afflicted personnel is just, and only learned minds can see the outcome ignorance feeds the empty vessel i.e. ignorant minds. Mentality represent the effect of action, as in the things that we do every day, the sins of the forefathers, the imbalance we as a whole have collectively created through our free will. Congratulations are in order, it gets worse before it gets better, believe me it does – as we see only that of which we are capable of understanding – indifference as is the way of the 'in' part of humanity, don't we just lust that, indeed we do. A sense of place is in pieces and all above board before we go; today we play the daring game like pawns in an opening slave lane. In response for a win or lose for the favour of tumultuous applause, a pause appeals to us all indiscriminately. For the love of labour, wisdoms accessible to everyone in general especially the chosen few who do the things they do in favour of the law. Disciples intimidated by local protestors deliver the blow for representatives of new sanctities sacrementation of the one God or the Great spirit so close to spiritual immunity as one can deliver the blow to. To answer the call in a new league of its own is foreclosure on dealing with the devil – dragged into the world of knowledge and fruits of favour for the labours involved are far beyond the usual expectations of mortal understanding. Never condescending nor interfering with meddlesome masses, the backbone of consumerism all around the globe – despite the ferocity that exists out there in the world of our own making, there is and always will be a massive undertaking held before us. Yes indeed the battle rages on indefinitely above and beyond the call of duty – revolutionary construction is unbearable supposedly for cumbersome crews in need of maximum protection. Held together by an infrastructure so rare and delicate that its precious cargo is very expensive yet fully functional. Far advanced than prototypes of formerly formidable reputation – and thus is critical for our motley crew, and achieves its potential without hesitation. Far from invincible yet highly forgiving in nature, this extraordinary creation is supersensitive to changes in atmosphere and social consciousness and power of suggestion invariably. After all, accidents will happen won't they! All over the place, disintegration verses destruction in tactical manoeuvres never before imagined by ordinary citizens of the most unavoidable situations ever known to *personas non-gratis* – dismembered individuals plagued by unrest and disappointment in staggeringly large numbers. Keen effort is gratuitous and inspirational with a keen interest in considering trust in unique and very welcome ways – severe in freedom and exposed on ever-changing levels of expense and critical structure on a wholesome scale for flames. These incredible surroundings are elevated horizontally from medium of sculptured elements of meanderings and of massive change for flat surface and stark minimalism – their quality of light moves in lateral ways, ruin follows in design, more in keeping with such visual distractions and identity. Modular interruptions are achieved and have grown out of quickening water reclamation with existing time-consuming tasks laboriously and recirculation of our good ideas more difficult than ever before. Still sampling supplies heavy duties logistical nightmare of survival – that suits everyone battered by the winds scarring self-centred egocentric eccentricities; what an incredible view this is we have selected from hard landscaping straight silvers unusual beauty beneath the skin. It makes it worth the weight in maintenance and ironic duplicity – groovy ruin mimics dark shadows and reflections in a majorly radical way, thriving entertaining and blending together in subtle harmony, breathing relatively easy again with pleasure in the work and research for the end result.

Contempory terraces fantastic restrictions have reservations above reproach in trump card technology never imagined in conglomeration of the loose undone ends turnover – decade after decade apparently flowering vigorously with majorities separate in humours companion and attraction for prefabricated rebel varieties. Excellent form for classified variants and unusual definition most definite in completion for wealthy is the heart that's healthy is provided the fat reviews are sympathetically resilient – arched magnificently with lavish embellishments.   Adorned directly through trespass, and conflict and fraternisation with the enemy – star seclusion with execution and multiple convictions for their crimes against nature and estate. To equal the celebratory half-time boost we have awarded a spectacular reward for relegated tourists hitting a challenging target just one day before banning of serious fraud.   Higher orders approval of deceitful tactics cause major restructuring favour a whole new set of problems – moving on poste haste for a rightful place in the sun.   Whatever happens eventually to the memory of each and every one of us in the hands of foreign bodies, absolutely official in confusion and imaginary tack.   Aligned to authentic investigations now for image deprivation and damage through insurgence celebration a dream of an historic expansion for all.   Potential oversized voyage around the globe, an active instruction is in deep and well below the knees.   Then no chance of escape in this here place my friend, have to keep it moving, stay cool, talk to the hand, keep calm, don't get ahead of yourself at all, in anyway at any time for any reason you may find.   Avoid confrontation with charm in place and winner be with grace in tow – fever pitch destroys the pace, make great escape a tall order for anyone.   Departed has been thrown around without citizenship like a prostitute on a round-about easy listening for the early bird.   Performance takes an easy chance on everything it can; abuse of the missing forces allegation and how it plans to deal with genuine victims is on simulated report.   Launching to remember for portraits famous campaigns of quiet contest in dirty battle, now strong performance stains the green echoes of office and reflection.   Attack elections predecessor, extend this custom beyond the grave to deliver at admission or surprise the sort of undeliverable kinds of collusion we are accustomed to here in this land.   Without doubt sensationally insatiable appetite for sure of inexhaustible demure – a cure for unlawful conduct and extraordinary immunisation techniques never imagined by the ordinary man. Systems potential shutdown heightens awareness, installs a verdict and reaches accusations for all concerned.   Disruptions heavy and persistent press the right buttons particularly where wise surprise grows thin – the agenda tests deportation policies in the quarter finals.   Home is where the heart eliminates dark holes in record time – export stolen goods delivery of mass productions concern.   Warming bureaucratic hearts out of action completely before staunchly reacting through threatening induction techniques, for the spin off holds very big distractions in skeletal structures – needless display; official obstacles organisation of institution.   Gone to the jab and cross, posing for pictures penultimate compromise, we are sadly missing the point some may say, for this Jacobean stalemate partnership is devoid of any conclusion and unusual scenario momentarily or otherwise – burning stalemate drug dealing partnership forgone simulation in adherent formulas demise.

A veritable interface of chronic indignation, service calling sacred features, crawling in through spaces, fitting solid gold enjoy me, nearly there within that street where you leave it all behind in blinding moments glorious dent. Forth dimensions trajectories rejection, mechanical protection grinding away incessantly through intercontinental plates – thrust contention apelike exposé inner torment accusation. Fill us full of lead and first blood sensation whipping boy creation scum has eventually left the building, but for how long? We will never know. Valuable information for senseless generation that has come and gone long before sentencing begins – for everyone the same old game of structural anticipation. Amen halleluiah!

Chapter Seven

Pleased to say turnabout, take a last look at the part of ourselves we see the least of yell insularly outwards, removed will blindness be- executed heretic and lies and into the future breath again the peace of release and victory. Over hurdles of mass hysteria and blunder, enter beneath that passage so dreadfull and fraught with danger, come about face to face with the blank return of depth in a place of mysterious and yet of blissful existence, then back to the real world with patient blanketness to see the source and grasp metaphorically what will is done; not won. The power of choice upon the shoulders of giants , one step at a time for all to see- distorted images are washed away but just in time again for only a moments clarity in an uneven landscape stuck down with effortless movement and graceful craft against the entrance between. The stricken shadows fail only their counterparts in crime- echoes of dust fuelled encounters with the past, for more have failed where none have beaten; apathy and shame, would you agree? There is none that prevail more in times of peril than the eyes of wise men that smell success in dereliction and disorder, greatness is a spirit, it succeeds where all others fail miserably, creating a need for special favours and support when all is lost or won. Who will break the ice; where it is thin anyone can and will for sure of this I have no doubt nor do I care about it either- to add insult to injury where only the movement leads to rest from slothful slaveries demise. Indistinguishable from the word go, there's room for more at the razors edge with a hand held high above the rest, so far so good in this day and age- killed for the thrill of visible concepts eventual invasion or formidable resurrection. Done and dusted for the sake of raised spells bluish hue and charming editions ordinarily opaque confusion overflow in streams of white-lighted precious metal- vacant contempt leaves that special season to the hogs and hounds for a four course meal in flavours mild procrastination. Virtuous patience prevents scandalous ministry when anti- personnel device falls into places hitherto revised- breaking ball calls for closure and fearless fissures speed the pace once more. Poor louts with open mouths and lazy eyes revealed, calm down the breeding space and feed their bellies greedily- venturing endlessly through the centre of universal knowledge and eccentric central lucidities- heart and soul replaces blood and guts in immeasurable contest and concerned reversals in values. Influential conformities clear intervention forming nuclear societies where inequalities are rife with strife and poverties so blasphemous to the human soul we are dismayed in quiet splendour captivated- huddled together in guaranteed explanation for a miniscule projection complied in contemplated degrees of misinterpreted representation from rags to riches in senseless deprivation, closing the door of wild barbarism for good in thought and language from top to bottom in a flash of incensed bravado and of suspended agitation bargaining solidly for closeted extension to boil- for purpose to discredit the hard slog on distraught changes uncontrolled movement, to make a job of it; pure majesty unrolled. Satisfactions gardening expendable intensions extensively in all weathers for uneasy completion oil slickly extortions- physical affairs continue to employ fissure in issues farther than chemical intrusion endures. Sensed the bitterness and cold, engulfed the senselessness of control, drove away the confused mind from my darkened door to clear my own in the process, explained away the truth for the sacred sound of lies for a moments peace. A fantasy of flesh gives the game away, fierce and fast as hell where roamless roads lead to nowhere in a daze enchantments hazy shine and blazing dust-ball brewing up a storm for all to see; indeed-offering the plate of self-righteousness and self-appreciation after life-long struggles and indignant self persecution and dismay, devoured treacherously by cradle rocking hands of stubborn oppression and single-minded self-destruction of innocent hypersensitive souls for wisdoms bastard brother, those that slaves will never be, never ever ever. On the breadline federation simplistic degenerative diseases are impossibly sacrificed for the sake of immediate escape- literally shocking with undesirable effect of repressed desire of dire consequence and ritual scenarios anti-attitudes offence and fragilities. The truth denies responsibility, backwards thinking and larking in the park-disenchantment brainwashes the hell out of the underworld from intimate surroundings and back out again. Adulterous comraderie devoid of language or undulating gripe, a tour de force; gravitational indifference grows closer in uncultured disregard and uneasy lethargy for the sake of animus. Slowly offending academic dignity for sacrificial heresy in a supreme concoction of ironic hypocrisies – ooh that motive of nationalistic anti-puritanical servitude that sees the art of idiocy. Master and mistress in stricken similarities constructive cause and consequence seemingly strengthens in a sense prophetically paralytic yet cleverly ambiguous-serious psychic phenomenon fails to impress regular mortals to the bone indifferently disguised per se . Perfection never bothers to interfere with the polluted atmosphere of accentuated foibles insurrection and facilitated propagation of anthropologically morphed clone killers- power to the people where variety be the spice of life, plug in and play out; how foolish can we be where the call falls down around evil vessels as thin as the air we share. Don't get me wrong, we should pity the fool that both frustrates and arouses pitiful compassion at the same time as foreign it is to exert or retract a strange pleasure from their direct performance and free delivery. Bemused enrapture captures casual intricacies throughout the days leisure in somber mood restrained –unconditional surrender wipes the table clean and rest assured remains the same. Force-fed mind bending niceties of feathered friendships ever lingering odors in exorbitant abilities to extend demolitions order around the clock- power over the advisory's accapello crony mis-interpreter of the decade, get the point man? Improvements epic adventure impresario better watch out from this movement on, fabulously crafted and endless in its entirety and foreclosures conscience mentions more- far out without the weight of loosened grip and present function flawless. Faith caused stylish doom and high qualities intravenous rise in resistance all alliance kicking through permanently average savagery's declaration- dreadful accusations clueless revision and inclusive obstruction of hey- presto! Immaculata hermaphroditicola patheticas: monumental lapse of blindness. A stroke of good luck more than enough for slaughters ever-lasting ascension- open where the winds island is likened to itself rising about the sides black mountain hide-out stray. Bulling for a stretch thorn in your aside and hungers heart for raising hell in baited breath-cell rolls service Christian roots reach falling point- hurricane pushed wailing fresh showers home again. The skies the limit head rush rear ended generation shouldn't be allowed fresh-faced brainhead born to be alive- kicked out about lovers sides, strewn about the room. In touch with our blindness and bleeding behind us, solid gold plates for protection unwinding flash and learn to follow through in time for tea- chill time a callin long before the seriousness finds us frayed legless for the prefects gone awol today. Clearly diffused embraced probation and tame cohesion, base beat nationally identified perfection- tongues unidentified shamelessness virginal creation turned dry in the mouth all sameness behind us sarcasmically obstructionally flamed.

Insomniac tails methodical stories invites inclusion ridiculous voice-comic jest baited breath pours doorstopper lock stock passion marriage, gruesome twosome shower plays the blue tune one more time. Fresh blood for dinner and guess who's on the menu and it's teeth sinkingly thirsty for more curdling mercies-wonder pleads his case and values her place in the garden of indecent harassments reluctant recuperation. Sacrificed old martyrdoms recoiled instance calling cards how do you do these things anyway says the man- depth arrives just in time to leave us once again in chains of esoteric rigours. Chanting dust-like features welcome I from hidden places – wordless visitors from distant lands, vibrant echoes of the past searching for us. Standing old as time itself, for a stretch of the imagination; impact of friendship for the cause thank god but why so ordinarily subtle, is faith so far away now or fruitless labours escaped our grip. Rest in peace forever and ever . Rest in peace forever and ever until judgement day has arrived, there lies the aside, the edge and last stand for it's in the cards, the writings on the wall where pagan moths beat all mortal pulse and favour and to fall or even falter able-bodied youth and senile hag unaided to the mark enslaved begin the journeys western voyage home to the halfway house of the soul-ravaged and beaten by trespass. Gain the trust of ruling tribes; scribe can remember well the sound of angels flight in days gone by for all remember stories told of high adventure and of low endeavours cold grip on armour and shining sword soaked in blood the golden horde surrendered. There you have it closure on the brain rings true across the finish line running wild and in your eyes the heathen cast is broken -aimed well and true at the loins of mis-contented mainstream .An all inclusive optional confusion of the brain-all creatures must take a fall. Sound-fillers freak down and out in favourite ball-breaking sit-downs surrender morpheous melancholy- meridian lines will abridged be a moment's weakness escapes the price of leaving. It's a great pleasure to enjoy the slight of hand repaired; an extraordinary austere chapter steeled or blown to bits in brutal bouts reduction goofed outside off sorts-one hole town almost hits the rolling climb ejection seat emergency manoeuvre from behind. On top of the world one minute, then slam and crash we're on the floor for more the next, it's a cold and crooked world that's for sure-specifically stricken thud free-falls complex rides weasel-like rolling thunder sounds around for all to see. Least effort strays out of the way with each passing year losing it's grip on personalities different daze – without question a burning sensation slowly manoeuvres up the spine and into the space between the lines. A little strange indeed in warm embrace to ask of ourselves, cause and effect yes but what of what context to get to grips with it all in extreme measure, slow but sure never settle for less cast out and set in stone. -fallen angels excused from that great gift. Out of reach adrift on terrified torments inc. corporate diving head-first into the subconscious subterfuge after a night of menacing malevolence- piece by piece, bit by bit, it's a process of elimination like never before. Crowds of rowdy so-and-so's floundering headlessly into the throng of wrath fuelled wrong doing and recreational interference healthily ignored by the frenzied cause of sober intention and abuse-single determination minding it's business in highly justifiable regard though temporary sanitized relief is just honourable function main-lining profusely in function only. Horns on a sheeps head follow suit in carefree ways where all losing headless fever animals severe reaction stills the pointlessness of fate fallen angels favour their remission for a time of pace changing peace in exchange for scapegoats odyssey inactive change or precondition modified. Torso holds the fold of emptiness and fury forged confession chambers listlessness' pause and carefree more chaos in forced admission in sanctuaries temporal face the carved faith of merciless find grace. Floundering sorcerers lead the way forward in unison, together till the end of the road beats a clear path home again, tilling fields of virtue stick through thick and thin remorsefully inadequate numbers to brush back the opposition, all clear sailing ahead for now, baited and wailing tediously tail held high. Belief in luck when reef holds high the faith-entrained savageries of kind employment indignation spreads away a troubled scent of rhyme and rent-free reservation- what a feeling of coarse multitude and severed leech ordained relief, the common cold treats us all the same at last we're even jockeys I! Calm on down at last or should I say least it's for a good cause, freedom plays on –fourth dimension courses through my veins again flash- flood carnage forces open streets of change like stretched out libels ornery procastro mourning after-halos peal. Personal traces injuries verbal incompetent monuments of equal measure harder than steel ordinary sibling weird instilled frail ponderings lead pipe fortunes oily introduction to any tradition or sentence lengthened strayed essential force invention- cruel knight of astral order heaves-ho in time for struggles lain blast rage doctor soul to soul strength or strain. No holds barred domination needless to say insane creation shepardley scent-matched position proved-closed dealings forge the way ahead in comforting bliss and chance encounter steeled. Original moorings torch the bailing southerly tip of sound and fiery temperatures, olden goldies cheap ambassador of ingenious sense and service- here comes mucho madness to the strength of change and torment ends again-whisper of the wind Open wholesome domain as action rears it's ugly face then strakes across the sky salivating greatly for everyone to see. Running simple tears drop from the eye cries out for more of the same auld mockery; run aground –whisper of the wind clears the air and shares the outdoors evenly. Bludgeoned fathers ancestry, national heritage renewal of essence flailing spiral inspiration- bare bones open door therapies, back-to-back politics cave in ominously, first time follows on through in scraping to clear action by no means an easy slip of the tongue. Advantage hides the inevitable race of suicidal traditions brave in the attempt and cycles reason for leaving diets new diseases-stamina dares to gruel the trade on time to rumble trade and sickness beating. Major stroke of luck slick and easy trained in fiery spread and foresight informed inner circles miracle escape crucial to the taste of fate.

Casual reflections personal example of strewn salvation processes paste-like tissues grey circular detection and mass of volume sample exhumed –specimen causes cure in cool and kind parameters renowned for high prowess and lack of cowardice defying death impressively woven. Stationed alongside some extraordinary persona non gratis of extreme idiocy and walks of life in general perfunctory talks obtusive mile ahead of rest and rescue –fall reason tall proud confrontation obstacle grind stop fluctuating masterminded abyss incapacitated bit of much chewed clever clogs and goody goody two shoes whatever. Weighed and cleaving shoulders first top off towards the watchful eye and something's nothing more than wrist twist methods breakfast teasing- one word at a time however way you cook the soup it's all in the eyes me darlin' and that's no. Have a little faith bud without change to flee from merry vents off-peak haulage pristine force to whisk out scrummage stories oh! Direct vessel storage systems freak their distance harder than before, a strangers present folly forces order on demented minds after the race was run; we have a taste of distant echoes boredom killer-soldier on, speedily deranged, creeping toiletries freedom march out of the chaste and weary tale of old ways; in disarray we collapse and hide our heads in shameless over-simplified injustice, carry on your mighty master does you proud. Justice balanced horse heads, sheep dipping humane caricatures kluk kluk plan, bragging dragons wade in swamp and shore heading for disaster- choosing it or chosen by the very thing that finds it's way to our door; painlessly introduced before the scars divorce from reason: to put it simply, just for the sake of self-preservation we deny ourselves the truth again and repetitively free more chains out to dry the well completely of hope to change- no faith, no excuses, it's over and out restaurant recuperation regenerated Christmas has finally arrived again for all involved the silly season has landed and it's time for the cold to croon at the last trumpet closes saloon door chaos bombastic basket case emporium relief- stories golden movement; just never break the mould when the only way is up and outwards boys and persona non-grata has the floor. The best we have are the weakest we can offer; the broken yet twisted knot of hovering lover love that's true-triggering shapes to materialise out of the thinner species horizon fault or folly enclosed on our behalf in order delay beatitude for Nile river the walk edging better on for bait. Included also the greatest feat of flavour stretches out the blue fire of birth pangs merry chase and innards he defies- imaginary functions flying questionable and content across the fear of undeniable race is out and of something steady grows-prison private gone for the helping man, break disgracefully and orgasmic us all to the depths cellular table for thirsty work in need. Keep the claim open for the time being, leave the boy cal up to me and watch the world go past web forsaken search for joy- decapitate them just for joy employed-sights before the eye contagious goblin years in foetal positions gracious. Midnight blue in vague isolation of another age far out of reach yet with us more than before- bone-close more and more to the marrow sworn old school door blues and warming in matters rightful escape. Slowly but surely the heart of the matter treads very carefully on jacobite skulls for erins sweet rescue within reasonable inflation, truth, same as before adores the silent shame of freedom. All blood split on these shores no longer in vain for this year the truth will out and clearly set the blame the slaver: in alls well ending present shallow failings, set us thoroughly free again, to the island once and for all the earths inherited. Always cusp the circles round centre heartfully befriended daily endured spread across the battlefield where spirits boundaries know no end, ivy handling fierce and powerful stands here, us and them apart and level above futuristic amendments cause is just a walk away down the rivers edge clears the head from illness shake hill brush will save clear rattlesnake the night awake frontal lobe risktaker born of sheepish eye mistaken- of ten breaths easy to the ridge in earnest. Folklore spoken costly ranging blue lagoon-like freezing sorted mad in the head and towel dried tender, monies made easily and dried out crossbreed quick surrender-strength in numbers foiled enjoyment strictly fed a slice of one detested flavour of incredible misinterpreted execution. Block and partake gripped star hold safety shoot behold and diamond in the rough once and again to shake rattle and roll enough is too far folded seriously been done before she flashes streets ahead of the packeted alternate universal entry- completely eyes on voracious eaters of stars electronic absolute trade off dead invincible gangland elation earth religion centipede funk or no funk falsified proper order indeed force or he is wrong from the off horn player queen in full regalia sorted something other than the heart of man. Ingrained animal passion and or zealous mighty sprinkle futuristic organic mainstream platonic keep a clear head before we all go up and down the cringing house fall drowning ice cold in a fix for us all endangered planet pieced out in favour of the youth included- sound and soluble conditions empty out the regular form for a taste of things to come-the way things were it is better to be easy peace out, move on to make worse work. Long suffering tendencies succumb to the polished ground suffocation and more to the point calms it down opposite strengths overexcited stretch and involuntariness tollbooth blues-often the mistakes we make sweet cat paste heathen enter the massive desert sand, close down completion extremities. Cornocopic creative testimony to those that invite surrender caused cohesions laughter, all are eventually splayed turnarounds minty fresh surging wave splash deleted block- strayed path bounces back lonely beaches black attack volcanic dirt is dust cosmic delight even and divine sun tribes beak beauty joy surrounds emotive shape expressive music natural form level beat soul hand keep more sting tales level and kidnapped princess ultimate starved footroad paths life-never-ending spirituals liberation mourning perfect instrument remain plucked percussion hammer lyrical penpoison improved rock rock knock tan warm from the sun; one won over. Avenged in equal measure flat faced in disguised mode undeservedly so- for more of the shame twisting exile po-faced casual frailties exile of the decade smart-alec.One more blank stage coach expresso fragilities take it easy Japanese karma cola frenzied enemies just for the joke in deaf, dumb and fined barking mad extremities favourite year in the life of bordello inferno remedies question many special: depends on the outcome more or less hidden from refined eyes. Wherever the penny stops my friend there's only one way out for this poor sod pagan Christ and all in tow to swap a charging bull when torched so much so- grunt and groan the oven door breaks outward, low and behold the wolf circles around pacing splendour back mighty album home sweet home the forest beckons first blood surrender gender federally in expectation moderately out-sized trial and error partakes in the earlybird menu for a touch of classic innuendo far before tonguelashing vacuums hold on to their festival appendages-freakish birdcall trained all-star bulls blood floorshaking headroom insiders cast in rubyred shoulder-length fetishism acropolis. In your head spread out on the farm toiling tensions stateside ominous and sword-side right on, follows the code chord and scales broadband electric colourscheme on draining untoward enigma slice wound about the crooked indentation belted bootybotting blessed birthright. Same as every other thing that corresponds to many times just buzzing blondie babe in strange detail sage respond to stimulating growths freefall- for this weakness you will fall and live another delayed decade, refrain supposed to rainy draining flaw and flaking nothing's wrong with overcoming obstacles one at a time. Give break rest-give it a rest please phase out the silent message please invade this gentryfuelled scenario for pearly birds of prey and generous ledger helpings rest laid paste shade frequence shallow sadies sacrum blade infernal frantic jasper bone. Giving up the nicotine ain't easy but it's worth it man, it's so hard leaving it all behind at the end of the day- to see what extraordinary people call everything takes an everlasting flight into the unknown flesh inconsistency erstwhile drop-zones into forest fray. Foiled love and spirituality lets taste discern polished fixation in tasting times, Mayday memorandum- that's what we all like to hear. Be whatever you need to be until the trees growing's and fly away- go away, leave, return no more, for any reason, begone from here, get out here- night-time is calling the strange unavoidable countenance leaves and breach in hull and begs in withered pageant pledge for easy patronage still addiction gains the eye of wrinkled brows common string and the ripple crest of uneven territories, the outcome lies in this balanced grin-sooner rather than now, tempest weighs me down and slips easily without ceasing for a moments rest to take it easy crown like slow punishment and sceptre hand in hand and pause growth hand me downward floozy vixen sheepily grown in thorn-bush teasing wistful frown. Peace finds excitement from nobodies business, yes indeed dream lesson number four, there's so much more than shell fortune faker fuse for every little holding speech impediment doctor seclusion never tired talking spirit ask me please into the centre with you so; go belief system through and through threshold- let bonny pace ease into the place, lead down, out-seen free-back strong hit foil tiller exit.

Cauldron of plenty fill our hearts with glee thank you, live life heartsleeved one way or the next, wing word falter flight just slightly out of sink, think bright thought righteous Ethiopian maid Demolition blindness surveys the proud verb resurgence eventual substitution of the whole king shaboodle , bursting into a fine unknown territory where muddy water runs deep shallow shock dumbfounded inner world including mention patience virtues in vertical limits haitian. Doubt sets out find metaphysicalities munchin' crunchin' climbers fun to mention of distant frog heaven, it's definitely a thrill to kill the mocking herds angry jealousies pertinent strain for toys drooping safeties and stone lizard pain reckless fridges funny fountain slow. Thorned saint cosmic hive far street bar below, off ranting wildmen hillstruck pill plucking ravens hair again- nothing to dedicate this spacedout master of ceremonies too, driven hard wasted colour coded inner adulation sacrificial scape-goat floating prayerboat wrings the neck far into the night burning candles out to win the bet and single shiner sin. It could have been the very last night of your life and painful to the mix, who can tell, these fixhead things, no-one knows what dreams may come from this- long ago and far away, painful merciless absorb the stress coarse and ready mixed warnings warm embrace wears a friendly face why not just wash it all down to the back of the throat and single outsome residue for the boatman's memorial ceremony in silent solitude or vacant macabre for the sake of a dime on each eye. Tick- tock lock horse-drawn greed killer flight of the bumblebee shake it all over the hoose goose clear picking ranging towards edge even keel severe reproach common coachman's marvel –eleven songs pristine circle elvin green mistaken identities bushspike spiky thorn sworn handshake black mountain goat throatcut hand drawn self same guts spilled out floor tooth eyes n' all in awe of war! Another way to foil the fodder, soil to yer song and bounce that bother bring to the boil there's nothing that makes any difference in wanton threads divorce and artistic merit down by the swanny rivers flow new growth we giveth joinery. Meticulous interpretation saunters past grave grammatical aviation- sheepishly divorced to aside error riddled with childlike subtleties elasticated bridal gowns of course. In hesitant supply the hemp is high bursting from extinct ubiquitous embellishments call to leave here and fast as you can go without delay or any mood swing swore. Luck follows bright sparks devilishly close swizz cheese chose for more evil twin whosoever swings the more measure mostly flash he is on lightly feathered ground of a sort. There're is marginally thin yellow sound faltered far before the line of she is on foretold mean centred fountains youth full persuasion impresario invasion of the fences spent obnoxious rummage toomed on toadbed boredom blessed hissed fist mention or tails stressed, get offa me crowd 'n' gas up the mess tear awake stake a festival venture through the known regions best sailor legions far tail seal of hope reef hill a proof hail oh preened Madonna shale they saint ewe. Tours my or all we veign sure, fails to spit on river reign moor toll height-full hex ecstasies burned black minx tail on the hound drain summer shore crystal remedies unfortold alliance fear of flying in the shade of things that may be detained, drained and cleared away without a doubt nor orange soiled thane sunshine glen. Blame it on the great game as evenly it passes by- greys called race reform drive slightly out of sync and stern activities rise over the red blooded plateau to southern cross it's way about place, where ere we go. A natural grace sullies heavens willow branch haven coveted ground trial effortlessly sleeping outright valley road below sad Neptune's tremors- dark and cataclysmic joke hers is wander lily poe-faced floot farcical, in box I gate hit slow in the water too irate we go, all in or rugged Father Joe confine mentalities distortion. Waiting crystallises braveries tender length or waste the taste of rich reward some more idolised freemasonry sees daylight hours more done- strenuously occupied instant karma qualified fleshtivities instrumental solitude of more denial in varied existence on an even keel squalor and reason lifts us over sides entrance clever cheerful live performance jolly growth. Firing boiled lobster pots singed flavour tiny tot, sorry vestal throne rises or drops into the stony river, for the dew has lifted, the frost is gone and we're a sorry sorry lot all the shame say I it's true. A fully fledged theatrical adventure of domains well bridled secrets, for the halter holds the spit in hands clipped salty and dew lined banter splintered wise meander thick insipid fuel and candles lit for horseman this way comes in harsh weather spit- orders of a sortee maiden comb black here grip handles hold womb together grained shalom this hardy tribe alone forever. Travellers rest climb high together gather solid past and present pleasant sentence wind and treasures past are wet hindquarters of break spit for lengthened friendship lions share and stay course nor spellbound leather purse that's worth the toil hereafter. A tempest rests it's weary head faith heal this cursed sideshow froglegs cycle go broth breaker step sholess shattered frail and tease. A tall wind grows- the terrible tease calls birth distance edgeways-forthcoming journey frozen. I cycle far and wide through castles doorway open window sooth evasion occupied the lance of sombre devilry and chose the pangs devotion- luckily there lies our mothers mixed emotion text and virtuous tardy legs will carry waves caress and begging forgiveness slaves thank god for rest. Sigh for a second, wave fare thee well to flesh and chemistries delusion- the third pillar holds forth the quarter now and lives well this brief halfway house remorseful wailing wall to falter propheteering meddlesome muddled madness in whole existence life towers in the sky hold mountains eyes fixed well on solitary doorsteps antiquation- Theirs is the house of prayer and at last ! The chance of wishful dreams academia still. Nothing desired but spirits pouring knowledge wisdom and practical philosophies to beat the band- how long will it be when revealed woven artisans come ever clean handedly outboxed to share clear crystal cheer together here and there whatever. Even warriors get the blues over one thing or another- their wisdom is in waiting and temperature gauging, fruit of the loom bears down luminous from ledge lords in discriminate decimation for a few dollars worth of thin that is more than expected idolatry. Drive out the wasted wrath when empty heads are set upon ground level haste and warn our own ways back without a hesitant crying wail for wall of wailing bearing fall. See that oil will smelt the metal of that doom forgivement hollied end and pass the lowest life out scapegoat burnt in sun torched desert looming feather ravens claw lacklustre free for all season rigmarolled joker and pestilence more to them that look outskinned holy; more scorned she is that destoys all fallen angels, mice and men. Pied piper play for us your mighty magic whistle now while all who listen see shapes academe blossom; mind hospitalities- spearhead powder flash amazement some more tyrant trade rise up tomorrow waits then again each straight purities victor spoiled encountered redeemer released east. The revised version of events causes to develop escalate and alive oh absolute complete subtleties, bodies beautiful size involvement works it every time as per usual- charity they say secures pursuits in former friendly far away places. Don't walk away from me my angel. There is change tap-dancing it's way across the stage, lost track of time however you look at it mother; The samurai is projected through changing worldwinds cross mounds forgiveness please and now It's time to leave but only for a while. More complaints restrain this secondary feudal territorial existence. Far more than before oily censor shapes abscond before our ill at ease consented carbon based elastic folds resorted violins concerto orchestra- move the dark slightly too and fro cradle labels mudslides overtures limitations blessed curtains down and out crescendo into actual mechanics and membrane mercurial testimonies ended triumphantly. Central gratitudinal mention movement invocation peaceful perfect meditational remembrance deviation-transformal tradition shapes up for the crowd in full sight of the shade or case wise auld freezer creature incarnate morsheeba horse goddess fears the crowd co-habitual chorus wheeze there you have it cracked erasions dormant episode smooth as the breeze blowing in it. For all to see a dangerous current is here below tailed serpents massive beacon suffice said frantic vibraphonic vampires connotation same farcical philosophies give and tactful familiarities careful as feline fountain ferocities melancholic surrender to the greater catapulted pupil Egyptian priestess named still sand god be reign high sky flight delighted it's a cliff-hanger folks high octane stock 'o' nonsense mortal spoiled egad ! He towers first devour thin edged blade, tis as sweet as choky pokey pie from one angel as one another may calm be dependable upon thigh optimal scented priestesses sceptre storm across the sky in spoken falseness melodies. While the least of us puts through it's paces all our place and acrid charm the heart of a man is all it's worth gold minion arm: treacherous brother marked right wailing truth be be decked out shore failed tried torc messed hip swath perform hate sealed amour adorned from taking form adored sect in other bleeding costume worn out festival peace eazy street toe bloated wee formed maligned caricature documented date saves it for the staged life born to fate a slave robed satire sold again of doubt. Bad news hurts the freight train provocateur, incision voice pulling fair question later soon backs uproar heathen yellow bellied vixen bard decision problem personnel -dole out the feel great discharge papers on the boil behaviour, severed bedside bait, cheer kingqueen misbehaviour bodily harm screened in porridge bred detention beaten fatally final. Blasted continually crater victim hospitalities strained report of critical consequence, offshore revenue correction generally racketeers damned perseverance inoculated device and residue- systems high pressure reigns on high flatlands shipwrecked havoc showery fall these bits and pieces on our governed mountainside vocation.

Tempers flare in an instant hell breaks loose; there's more to life than idiocy and self-important egocentric illusion of improbable standard for cause-afterlife flyers trail effort well below the game free for all topics of discussion morphine oust that creature well before their lamented tunnels favourite twist better below wasted tune for survivals limited progress.

Take you to a higher level far more than before still heart beating devilry quick dervish damned upgraded performance remediate- slip four grade from ninety superiorities installation raised today escapade hit and run tactics stock insult is made re-run. Friends and loved ones hasty flesh fiend teacher windpipe the question begs the answer north of the border in our rock 'n' steady bitter shine for all heard 'n' sole finish quiver sleeping gave her liver rolling times request salvaged trunk and ship destroyed together all-strongly focused terminal incohesion surgesforth crisp and clear to bail towards shoal scores affair, quit quite and bragged out industrial velocity for all. The great collision throngs decisive victories more than enough for every Irish trail excuse endeavour screaming out weightless abuse- uneventful culture bothers strength in tepid skulduggery volumes extreme exit acceptance strange transmission terminal tex downshift line flies on bye heads; approach bent code sector approach their edge is drooping down playbacks beat the band for a unique isolation supreme inbound extrudition act – on order, swat team furls abuse and handles the situation perfectly balanced intuitively. Weave away their sin it's all the same breath easy from the mark for working mechanisms barking up the wrong tree again- so there it is just like it's always been, rarin' for the marching other peoples braveries, tastes better all the same fire bails water boils southern sails falter toiling coils in stained bigotry glisten forester braggart then lists aside too bad- sorry to hear the soothing samples of democracies player vertigo idolatry infinite possession justified solace jail for life baby. There is how in the name of God do you expect people to go ahead and understand what the hell you're on about; baby face yourself, video seen crazies, moron you ran dumb, bay yes toe fear hill, your loose, he yin, eat and that's for deaf in hate. Foreign abacus core tune bill beat tamed fear cabascus pore fussaroll arcadia- nonsensical verbal fuselage that now ceases for fear of non publication and spokenword complete isolation, I mean come on Penguin can't possibly comprehend consideration of illegibles, can they? So welcome back legitimate literature honey buns, amen! Careful, careful my man they're listening, watching clamped well before market prices fall, pudding bowl classic termination of the path, halfmark fruitcake weeds best man blood vessel comediennes condemned from the start astray once again. Biggest letdown of centurial match four cascades and seep from the soul special partnerships grab them sleeping with the enemies downside brakes on, in and sights boot too avoidable. Boat floating parasites parade pick me up- legs eleven tries too hard, works on straight edge paradoxical. Practical remedies current social pick-me-ups deep conversation: too swear bailing squalkbox. Jesuits great set sail on ghostly entrepreneurs peerage and protection kingdom registrar. Vicious social injustice calls joint decisions trial and error: glamorises societies message to the local substitutes inaugural dialogue gangland raids vigorous and brazen prohibitive response to treatment- Bare absence vicious also deals keen busyness for everyone involved- organised heavy hearted routes runs up enterprising tabs respectfully way worse than can be understood by the ordinary man alright! Day after night fearful of misadventure demeans midwestern philosophies everywhere- other broadback underworld freedom dealers attract defiance alone and unassisted identifiably devoted only authorised on order detail charge contradiction. Individual coherence relates matters more messy than before told fortunately over time so sure of ourselves are we state jester abusing tenderfoot comedies sizes out the competition in martyrs memory stronger than the truth or dare friction favoured by the periphery preferred intention. You are the apple of my eye in respect of the past employment intercession violence down and over productive reasoning abhoration liturgy deliberate on alternative remedial presence popularised and readied for the countdown of the century immaculate. Nothing from nothing means something survives the caste system in some way otherwise personified - interference represents seasoned ripple effects on the heart of the matters quake and shudder flexibilities surmise supreme deliverance chivalry. The riches reach beyond the grave and far into the future tenfold reminding us our fate slips over mortal men cracks 'n' all- unbreakable from first to last as long as persona non gratuitous spill beans and all force amazed and frail glamour reasoning. So much toil and trouble makes sense of sanctuary- no idea possibilities excellence outfits version true neighbour hails slim fit trails away fear foremost slavery. Adrenally perfected fuel for poetry restricted- illogical solution seems too irate for the soothsayer's conduct and irrational temperance of behaviour supposedly commonsense of the herd kind. Needless to say there's a strange freaky stench of l'amour hanging from the racist tree on timid tendencies from one way next and other ways extending outwards- broken complication for normal discrepancies ordinarily unkind, remark calmly step in toe substitute and arduous task remain for infinite timid reassurance arbitrarily midget sized portion: breaking up the excellent manners in complete scenario- sentence or voyage, who knows? Beaten post-mortem riggermortis celebration slight of hand from head to toe, is this the eye of fragmented objectivities construction here there and everywhere? It doesn't make biological sense singularly foretold nearly to extinction humourless live be astride as can be dignified. Standard velocity eliminates straight standing accounts somewhere blood lies even, sister of havoc kicks oak tress in the shin: dismissal never lives long around here that's something. Hellish contradiction, degradation and hypocrisy fuels commerative lacerations interested in useless names tri-polar dominance fearful backwards stance- finished tidy sums collected cerebral stammer for arduous ordeal in taste and all out squalor jest emancipate the manner hastily retrieved oral defence for all. Definitely one for both personages of the accident of choice behaviour- excuse me for bothering to mind my own business mind over matter dysfunction inner turmoil pressure of peerage now in session- wings overdrive take a back seat red light alright sunshine. Strict discipline shears wool off the camels back just for the hell of it junior- wherever escape cruelly denies us our inside information, there lies infamouscies master of celestial rancour bucko. Orchids anti-doping rules annulled longwave flowering thinks paradoxically about the future woe betide- blooming hybrids species settles for a mixed source for membership return and of international correspondence unilaterally divined alternate conditions reactionary and variable direction calls forth preparational legislation on factor fiction insitu all the way- highly speculative tongue lashings are coveted xtraordinarily by each recipient. Larger than life yellow cab action super continental science backs up all the way- on the surface evidence has wiped out all opposition temporarily twisted in most situations. Apparent circumvention drivels down deathbed confectionary involvment- heavy loads crack out the champagne. Serious head injuries hold effective prospects in effect of charged sustenance in transit dispute of pathological threat for resolution- intervening novelties assist in slackening loyalties apologetic performances. Unprecedential organisational pro-active expulsion, celebrating centenial exploits; premature evacuation impulsively fortuitous convulsive fits etc. plumes and all Holy wars echo imminent dismissal of violent concern for nervous attack on sensitivities. Incensed falsity estimates proof of criminal activity on the aspiring meddler's actual physical plain of in errors- soul food relocated vocally inside and out so far and wide there's room to roam incredibly and rightly so. Powder to the people flash in the pan undulated candidates future swindle barking mad crescendo cyanide poison Cinderella's remedies dark secrets past and present- stay to course invention play decayed imported caskets placed rocket fuelled emotion, high listed memories thrill. Reasonable vixen hides the blame a hussies questionable intention scores fare thee well- extortion wears weary welcome home alone fair and square in greed agreed then spent again fervently advantaged in design remains. Pupilic relativity creates micromanic procreation: condensation proliferate tradition- make manic inspiration unindurable to shake the house down in traditional method only. Substitution marks out the beauty from the beast in equal measure each to their own positively armoured - induced productivity pardons the blood from the hood and the black from the word of our secreted organisational mouth. Beauty comes from within wherever yea may be popularised passion bleeding sulphuriously demoted perfection peers reflections fired up to free-social sobrieties resurrected melodies charm gives out perilously to everyone of inescapable witless intent and bumbling inferiority as complex as it may seem peace opens wide arrested development and sits out servitude velocity for artificial complacencies exit from the new-age airwaves remedial franchise of self- servitude- victims colossal completion exercises it's right to partake in submissive tomfoolishness. In festive season dribbling soviet garbage contrives anarchistic bureaucratic dishevelment red army chieftain privileged disarmament or group disorder. Dancing skin and bone Polynesian archaeological artistry finds another exit- wide commanders hidden Palestinian rebels active trickster wolves forest sinister breakfast on their layered combinations rant and raid brave elevation, labour fixed majorities; priorities in order. Guilty in a scented phrase content who weaves away our plain dissent for free and dominant comely made in chin or faith defeat an ordinary life. Certain complications bear appeased by ruler Venus marred- still there blocked roads forbear an undulating love for God and self unmeasured flowering shadow. A vexed head causes no liver, speed toward the horizon and leave the rest to shameless and unavoidable loss- subtleties infraradiation

Covers copies of it's kind, a wasting hindrance winds over hunters cauldron. Grammatical eviction overrides gouging philosophical recommendations in ordinarily transfixed seclusion- marginally frantic impulses predictabilities are gorgeously filled yet formidably evicted from occupied tenancies crib. Further from the truth in seer sized overdrive radiance hydrologic solvent bigger is better out protesting finalities distraction or massive ideology in evil liberalized fundamentalism and sickness fortuities- upwards onwards forever supposedly good god shepard goat herding many never be the same again, suggestively. Luxury patented airwaves lead the bill beneath the doubt lies energised afterburn entirely triggered distressingly and moderations curveball libertines deflamed.Laziness overcome by doubt filled anxieties infiltration or recommended vigorously in restless achievement ruthlessly personified - fear protects the beastly unproductive creakingly over fallen desperations eclectic pause for insult intake or vertical incline shoeshine jobs for the boyos medicine. Blatant black is back tenfold eazyrider all the way goof is cold armed soul food alligator chain-gang rhythm 'n' roots whole mess on- leave the man alone stranger it's time to go, move on. Each turn of the wheel separates somewhere freight finalities temperate tearing pick up the pieces bearing stimulating chant and charm-screaming fortification arrives timelessness covering careless constraint. Beautiful portions chase away the blues closer to the bone as avoidable trophies crown late groan-moisture feigns visitors housing collections oyster catcher ruminations flunkies shock prevention gnomes. Growling thunderous magi fall right before our eyesight ravenous archways caricature and natures own compliment background breakers raid tooth skinned- wait out stranger then begin the life's round return escapes all aeon therapists danger in essence. A holistic tradition saves fortified terraced flames crushed serpents compelled elevations in mighty storm and struggle provided merrily survived- rejected terminations cruel shot-put shortage predecessors abolition carved in doubt and consular temptations exorcism posed. Dissention glowing high fidelities airbrush maximum hardware flowing and normal eyesight sequestered Tolstoy carbuncle ready when you are ladies and geminies- better than the rest a race tasting query question greased up feline charm legion rectified. Lover leisure lends trailing saddles backwards aside pour play sure, in signed vexations omnipotence- authorised and estimations superior observance caricature pedigree secured. Signalled several credence occupied piper season savings session glorified head 'n' shoulders above third encounter aquatic division record holders surprise-twists and turning observation categorically devised the driven mobile correlative better for worse arena. Eyes meanwhile are downswing combining lifted token shaving anxious to the left length surfacing pretext printed spherical elation. Perspectively constrained deference's of farcical chop suey rudimentary production on-line alchemist tribal gratitude's- miles ahead of the game, strangle on gambler gig millennium staggered premonition regurgitated premonitional expression or contented measure poled. Labour tries to chance pursuits distraught surprise in adulation of canvassed propositions- frenzied fabrications vulnerable exploits employ common causes extra sensory perception. Intolerable circumstances precedential cell seekers, illegal authoritarian states easy pickings, criminal organisation covers all- first of his kind spotless tyranny prized possessions village idiot idiocy. Double trouble divination repetitively locks the door on both sides. Oh me oh my surprise what on- will I won't I snatch mark honest bloodlines foolish mayday surprise. Anxieties furtive ministry aviates olive grove blindness- inquisitors internationals euphemism speaks boardwalk banks connections radical qualifies entrance back out of the rat race and into step against the mould. Taxied station static comprehension, pre- enzyme inspiration gets gamey then mailed out- jasmine and ordained yet cast in stone forever sampled bested be forsaken. Stranger than bizarre, distanced caviared high speed memories- impossible and harsh qualities reverse slash and burn techniques medium vocation fermented triumph shares the vibrato via Mexico wave catlike minx reserve- risen from the grave long before the rain questionably stark handled validities return mademoiselle leans towards the grain. Subservient zero maintenance proximities coverage peaks about chance encounters- ghostly dealings silent witness malpractice break a waterfall together grained one thousand times. Exist in a gentle place slow 'n' shout hall speak ill aviary whisper toadstool eventually- bureaucratic requisitions fevered unusual tropical meltdown features compositional temper. In receipt of painful extraction, collaborative patterns and killer fast reflex co-ordination- set down relevance instead of neighbourhood extraction and doctored busyness lucidities upset. Chased guilty parties wrong doing dispensation murder paroled questionably sanitized yet necessary invention; districts risky outer hemispherical professionalism concludes the goal extreme and desperate. Sorry is the likeness voiceless your exclusive incision kingly guardian- roman physiologies termination materialises decorative fabrication for universal delicacies silky smooth induction and durable scar. Essential transformation creates tribal root clannish painstaking design wars on impartialities haven hood and pleasure pure luxuries-dispersed violence and liberation set list premonitions exit preferred interest offerings command. Crucial inclusions injuries doubt foolish meanderings tough 'n' stuffed achievements heroic intrigues barometer shelved- hope complacencies edgy opportune favouritism settles down to and fro. Checkout streetwise welfare scenario familiarities cluster shoal, elsewhere saintly lovers slack drift indistinguishable changes blow wind blow bright temperatures weak surrender- long time no see evolution civilization failed secure culture generation age of space indifference. United cowardice famous force persuasion leftfield campaigns normalities insult common casual and informal exclusion- royal innovation sweeps away apathetic indifference confidently complete. Sweetened alterations mesmerick courtesan; marriage sounds off fiendish flatteries faultless circumvention-silence holds forth great beauty and impressionistic shades overtone. Middle natural force and the flatteries sustenance combined in rapturous example porcelined wealthy trades wanton place remains complete. Obedience plucked pompous and unmistakably corruptioned sovereign surprise-dualities sweet lagoon ranks demure contest at best, the joker tastes vulgar fervent servitude. Countdown crisis threw herself in front of horse in order to shine wimble wily waster warrior clear away the damaged monster thunderer- equipped in all friendship follies short foiled equation new simplest version foibles R.I.P madam we respect contention in adversity. Deceit blanks out the past petition vetoes effected narrowminded professed discharge- low-down hardball bureaucratic nonsense sheds conformity with stylish serenity, chances leave death to his destiny and flow. Lazuli graces fortification insomniac ill spoken frailities veranda novelties quotation serum spread Confucius sprays free- sustained luxurious caricature coincidental imageries contribution and perjured measure taken reluctance to perform. Sudden natural symbiosis prepared handle of visibility trades psycho-logic Hyde and Jekyll terminologies survival- full measures strength and durability's extraction is compromised considerably and invaluably fixed. Future generations fixed adventures creeping lizard wizardisms spike their tails in honest pleasantries cordial- socially adept liaisons unappeased internment wakes the dead for remunerative gains. Shamanistic repatriotic energies swallow whole civilizations blind: light apparently throws progressional historical connections longevity mentalities touchdown vicinity and essence bellisimo ! Noises coil in natural mannerism majestic and all too warm in manner blessed- according to her will, animal instincts alive and haunting compel story remixed vocal incidence perfection. To play with fire fun fear experience inaugural tremor conductive seam stirring phase of petrified terror fame engulfed- miniature microscopic mesmerism hardly covers exit wounds comely waif or otherwise: so overall caution must be advised.

Learned explanations are pronounced subfootage fluctuations preferably holistic opiates of meridianic magnetised energies- possibilities protected bilateral textual interload leaves us far behind, far behind the rest of us and the best of all involved. Numbed explanations changed percussion instrumentally stroke the cat and stoked the self-same pack groovy tunes run around lift me up immediate remedial tonic- exclusive restraint leave laborious trepidation and hooliganistic intoxication in exorbitant exit. Signals statuesque examination exemplified co-ordinates structures of pump orientated prayer odd dubious creation – education foolish breaks brings folly to the cradle's swift paradoxical minuet, hour and lifetime. Gangland gunstick rhythm 'n' rhymes express joy and practical expression logistically refused intelligible: to conclude portions perambulatory step through the streets sure enough- reload and hold steady profit: dictatorship inclusion reign the whole day through, groove and chill redeemed and still. Disruption interrupted continiously. Avoided defiance bullies face value absorption- living speechless divine pockets resistance down straight amphibious cream o' da crop sensation. Grapevine blockheads rake bitter embrace full trance brainstorm old religions make break power feel good- instilled timelessly confused regulations mount up smooth as satin select curvature elevation giving glanced gold moon son slipping nature the move on- deluge strikes growth pathological feathery footsteps studio confinements installation complex. Framed exhibits corner common pleasures placements and resourceful celebrative earnest bemusement overnight carelessness refreshments- surprised physical consistencies secure strangulations central circulatory markings end. Contaminated furnishings small incidental personages social standing strains outside edges rigourmortis glorified – diamond terrorised deflations Muriel impossibilities duration ruins shamanistic journeys enterprise functional fixational mysticism fortifies a sound influential biosphere of systematic dimensions- awful confusions differential dehumanising dreams become a nightmare for hussle junkies the world overhauled gambler sleep sickness insomnia. Heads are born to suffer profusely exorbitant functions: emphatically enormous eccentricities sheer abundance environmental modesties: exact systemisations furious sensations fortune hits the bullseye imperfectly devoted to the whole. Dialogue requests unreasonable concepts resurgence- rivalled circumstance extracts supportive retrievals enterprise and surrender. Obsolete fear of heights creating monstrous scientific hazards indefinitely final without the quiet- journey of disquiet rumblings order-line of silver generalisation followed by thousand island meridian moorings tale of torture disavowed. Provided glamorous and lucky freemasonry's conversion to the soiled liaison's accepted relief- insoluble blooming reversions mainstream magical mythologies compartments colouring enterprised beaker glazed physiological pretence or expertise. Counterfeit requirements speedy recovery captures credible campaign; inaudible frailities articulated emotion insulates devoted particularities of equal and regular restraint. I think basically in moderation and level one is far more substantial and essential than spectacularly impossible to attain- valley high mountain morgue below ignores the growth hormonal Sabbath vertebrae it's a dream come true today. Gross deflation will prevent stellular visions precise evasion freaks meetinghouse comatose perfection- selected natural imagery cemented semetic prevention permanently reversed. Two tones equestrian servitude intent kills holiday's instruction for a blind buffet- projectile decline evades capture completion for a rhetoric taste of insatiable cremation. Subcultural coil cascades this psychiatric assessment of highly contested restraint wilful advantage contagious- careful envisage spoils for the cure gentle peerage smooth seeker completion revised. Relished transparencies crisp 'n' clear straight ahead either way- leviathan signed sealed and delivered very efficient in many ways one at a time. Left-overs leave us numb forever more and that you can keep snug and warm tremendously—volcanic eruption makes way for a natural progression entranced connections memories painfree existence recalls to memories fall from grace vertical interruption- entertained like never before again seen as double trouble wishing floor moonside bubble double doors. Quit dehydrations scarce recital open nerve strays coral sea radioactive tide and video calm their ageless rage whirlwind insurance scam- sociopathic tremors silent separation freaks unavoidable actions caricature. Cat-like reflexes physician heal thyself running stones five star vacations vocational interview cascades towards the hole- pristine conditions command in effortless obedience delayed. Never know when to drop the dreamer's retreat straight outside organised exchange- fully equipped morbid and demeaning solid structures spiral out of control. Forthwith shortcomings boardercraving lists superimposed photosynthesis- rolling over positively joined together forever statuesque and notorious when temptation braids herself same massacre. Definition hard playback from casual vendetta holds the forced centuries tender hock house merry choice tried- against public demand a voice yields choice painful viceroy goblin tooth decay. Vex playful queries spiked lunch illness revelries- there is fit storage prophesy in a peachy mood reunion block. Different strokes for different folks diffuse potential stimulating busyness tireless and impartial to worldly risky alternative vilifications order safe passage between their skilled protrusion ordinarily havoc wrecked injustices scooter poles. Motormouth laid waste and tires so easily- follow the handling reckless road that red lines seasonal growth in town and country dubious clatter – change the record baby face the music and hold show for all's well that ends well drummer drill the holy flicker fallen chill burn the victim slow. Carried high pedestal fiend and fortune wicker man scream til scream vanish and open sewer moan glow- worm candlelight and torchglow dim: knight in shining armour glimmer, boomhandle twist and turn slimeout wasted choice derails, set sailing sunbeam. Lighter sized situations look forward to leaning farout expressionless and mysterious rendition- thinking places hairy moments of great coincidence sized out and ceased up religiously. Deep contortions cork-up musically mused Judas sponging observants of late devotions- shot from dangerous grounds potential problematics stringent grace extremities tragedy and passions possibilities geometric surprise reality. Registered colourings hungjury shutters out the coldwinds reflection in eye shadow's winking book of the deadman's grave for consumed rage inferno ballet of blind academic dread, such in such. Amused incredible structural integrity acts on impulsive addictive heresy- form direction rare misguided margins: entranced queens lower than thou and fights tempests animal accumulations transieince the same way twice. Portraits compassionate embrace washed out picturesque sized out abandonment- all aboard a bounding clairvoyance voyage of treason-like extravagance, enter dragonslair laid barebreasted savage forced not out of desperation directly elsewhere fallen even, tomorrow strike the hour of midnight calm expands. Donedeal sponsorship cordial, a maiden voyage of superior inclusion is void in each and everyway superior-for ends meetings brings second stage. Ignoring charter interference winding stair defferance bleak defections year of the dog- smiling terminologies refusal tells crushed nightmares and king and queendom lands; brave decay unaired to the breeding mark swears biding marketprices share welldowned privacies run of the mill evasion. Exceptional assistance questions investigational techniques proposition cures faithlessness imperfectly- latched presumably blindness erased suppressions automotive session opticalized isolations repetitively. Indifferent existence meltdown carries no-one everywhere else but homewards far from the pressures drop droning peerlessly onwards straight into the arms of God's love- unbelievable consummation mourning mirage global situation stimuli coverage at the ready. Vital diagnosis incurable restoration teases futuristic correlative tastes benign- unnatural cravings call for a celebrative festivity of mental brainstorming reasoning ill substitutes of grand interest and like reminders. Swing low sing high and low in measure mentioned melancholies for the temperature is rising ready steady grow- one hundred percent degree centigrade controlled decidedly envious from end to end decayed from dizziness. Going through the motions as quickly as you can- safe for the standingroom ovation oratorical notice quotation. Take them out one at a time if at all possible- backwards anytime of day or night islands ring around the chains insanities monstrous consent. Frenzied clearance of demolitive forces and quintessential portions evocation- superlative veterinaries collection Barbie shifting emerges from the course eventual theory questions mentioning. Entire regenerative diseases miracle solutions hero of the hour heals to the cure completely- renewal or seclusion leaves the waistline on line for return of burning colours friction. Expression of inordinate liaisons inopportune attempts delayed- supergrass cream and sour devours a wise limitation exonerated. Warmed aground administered application; embraced emotional translation, modified laterally incohesive diplomacy and drastic measures compromised- indigenous dilation from afar fountain wise: mountain in valley high spirit flight creative juices flagging séance bold in arduous task; invention nearly solid mask infusion eerie silence joined silver clamped hold. Emotional expose tries in jest for mostly solid overtakings – leave the past to paste itself more than stormy weather. Life re-routes constant purgeries doctored exit highways slow levels low-down with maximum temperature flared. Crimson fire spreads through ghettos: so closure strays brave vibrato gecko leave the lizard down and out- casual labour lists in carefree modular intent an arduous alternative lesson learnt. Careful plunder beckons little record label listens, rude interlude- supreme maturity make more sensational quarters scent of brimstone coincides with deviations kiss- leaves everything up to their imaginary visitors return. Poised to react evasive techniques with andaluvean knowledge, expertise- on one hand elusive yet inauspicious sly, acknowledging that subversive appliance of method caused certifiable insanity to emerge. Celtic dragon both dirty and also beautiful at the same time leans forward thoughtlessly: provocateur remover of adversary carefully capable in every way : onslaught professionally bent on warming up friction on both sides continually in the name of falsity and self-satisfaction. Priceless interest for defence and action of control and intolerable frailities of grandiose drive-time will reveal tempest blind trickster stories old and wise, coiling heretic foiled again tasting tested in full force drained, the coach comes ever closer to us all with small compromise downed the swallowed pride in lucky fortunes cry. Struggling complications arise from hesitant misdemeanour transference occupier's voyeur of discovery salvaged- extravagant stellar perfection expands tight controversies righteous retreat back through filth and fog of failures champion. Linger does that scented thorn of thorny pride endangered species cleansed and wrangled tight on time- big throned thronging mass of flesh covered bodies fuelled to maximum temper and slight reprimand. Developmental

arrest significantly overpopulated interview calls forth images undeniably indifferent and complicatingly perverse- elsewhere dire circumstance designs an order all on it's own for evermore preserved. Practised perfection suggests an overdeveloped sense of fear infection and ordinarily hard provocation- multi-talented head games international union of fallen angels omnipotent exit from the face place world of cold truth melody. Unpleasant as it may seem relieved inner voice learned escape Alcatraz and place or pace tradition really- purposefully strict and visually cagey in clerical constrained instruction hoax intention cut and troubles duties bound- leaving a trail of destruction and liberations forwards carriage and subversive thoroughfare an end to slavery loosed about the waist against their will. Sabotage of sanctimonious calamity, hallucinogenic ransom is placed strategically under surveillance only for momentary lapse of sanity's refrainment – holistic consort and diplomatic craft reeks havoc on their sensual magnitude. Villainous reason composed by baffling entanglement and uncooperative particles on rebounding busyness of sociopathic experience – risen challenges chosen on spur off mentioned partners perambulation dirty work check out pins and needles quarterly challenged then in kind mindless obstruction mortified – worlds apart an instrumental menagerie incontinence dog eat dog on loan or contract will entrusted sustained from grievous assault ordained. Controlled action breaks winding stair refurbishment for socialites reactionary response correctional facilities – ardentine qualities consistent descendants falterless flexibilities faultless vanity holds Faust's recent return of blessed percent of perfection protected. Left of caricature gravely error seizing practices – eventual changes starts focus changing destruction our innocence procured overcharged and energised gridlock cries   crisis overload – scandalous denial of ideals visionary madness for companies militia transparence or global inspiration comatosed..

Chapter Eight

Reckless revolutionaries movement exhibits talents of unrequited antiquity – sociological indifference triumphantly reappears acheivably absolute. Weather-beaten translations of social disorder in so far as the instrument receives – foreign friends contest for regimental refusals deflated and egotistical prescription. Demotive antagonistic preparation pretext under constraint digs deep in fascist fascination borderline – bitter disappointment gives little away necessarily longing limitations contradiction and counterfeit for witnessed forsaken thirsts. Growth voyeurism liberates thresholds negativities consumerist involvement – dramatic melodies report towards identities post-modern prudence rhythm of soul. Blessed friendship similar object response attempt to intensity lightweight dependence assessed – factors campaign collapsed implemented suspended reign on luminous reef. Patchy forecast first nation reflection distress transaction pictures earthly tender – fixated prison protest hungers stimulating enrapture for ancient race abandonment or counterculture. Grateful fiesta contemporary situation proposition suprematism vortex multitask force of the moment – constructionistic overtones galactic inclusive protection protest abstraction. Kind fortune destroys creative design signified politically instrumental – academician backbone survives this turned doctrinaire foolishness and vermin like experience naturally. Crackpots abandonment trails forth subversive research denially spontaneous and progressive – technological impersonality allows for assumptions neurosis cancer and final catalisitic motivation. Severe diagrammatical stormfest of multicultural fountain for single use and recognition – recharging formal transfiguration corpsed deep below the line of usual scenes. Documented system of investigation provides criticism in searching points – artistic theoretician philosophises faces facets overtones ideological formulation. Intentions spirited response resists ingenious aesthetic relevance revealed – significant selection of discriminative celebration valuation and denial. Periodical interior that symptomatically drives outlimited editions glorified entrance into the next millennium – chaos theories perfected barewinded geometrical in shapeless reflection. Multifarious objective aspect proposes recognisable content contempt for compromise – aesthetic corrections derive paradox whispers enough permission spontaneous eruption. Shallow waters run rather flaky narrative conceived – directly rubbed declined photography resting traditions mortified metaphysically wired. Helter-skelter support in direct force in peculiar profile and expression manner and lifestyle – sordid scope searches heavenscent professionalism belated personal effects established.

Joined of the hip of self-portrayed material solvent in deviation revealed – distinct preview if applied verse richly yielded formation. Hanging basket raids fortunes sixth sense cultivation in order to evolve – emotional interpretations planet recovery packs permanent proposals punchbowl. Mental disease intrudes beautiful verbal impulse for sibylline pronouncement cordial – detailed consideration disgusts northern areas dry omnipotence and chiselled patterns turn for discovery. Mocking thieves' eclectic mist moves smartly outwards remaining body and soul apart – forever putrefies captioned conned exterior below the belted fury. Profound like resurgence in architectural velocity in harnessed sonata – proclaimed forksout beacons barebald consolation pedestal. Freaks how vibrato formation distanced from this global federation – lasting relapsed right out of horseshoe conqueror carriage. Defamation anguish luxuriousness desire flanked blanked out double doubt infinity enormousness – forgotten blues tune sentimental arcade intransigent childlike projection prophesised. Catastrophic crystal clementine saphron sapphire comments steely straightjacket – sooth sayers revelation divinates foolish anatomical conversation. Owlish fractures revealing large obelisk like transference defeation threatening provision – codexpansion trivializes presidential predictions decisive moments victories. Opulent misadventure forks out historical lament solution essentially sordid – co-existence glorifies the seasonal detention revealing original myths. Letter of the law enforcers flesh fantasies decision flawed remorse – convulsive exertion legioned bracing fatal specifics afaced dissent safety-net spectacular. Rumoured regret remembers contracted volumes traumatic escalated version of events – western warning counter attacks these most difficult queries unseen preventions. Irrelevant instinct encounters battered capturers ascensions decisive integrity – wherever something's found traces disinfectant legendary memories. Prometheus ultimation prevents solitudes drowning optimist persuasion – Armageddon's drifting south for now consistent beneath known fortunes burial mound millennia. Completed convention great sway futuristic variable sketch vacation – early years momentum beautifies contempt for unusual position. Studio vocation fakes purposefully through external physicality decomposing static and void – particular sequence interviews rapid publication full emphasis forgotten literally inspired. Body and soul figures fallen heroes influence celebrates functioning innermost direction – platitude of convention purgatives silent strategies honourable companion. Invariable surface method casts aside progressive testimony wherever it can – fulfilling engravement linesout intaglio methods smooth surface illustrations macabre tale. Black bargains motion of sale decorates diminutive perfect superiorities advanced antiquity – for loin saken simplicity obtains printed connexion probably typed with steady pressure. Linear subjections with intent falls on down temporary temptation forcibly corroded attributes in effect crosshatched – dissemination indulges the remaining monumental iconography. Descending occasion straightsided description vollies fleets sculpture pergamon renewal supremacies earliest betrayal – case closer to pointed negotiation throughout ordinary shields tradition modified. Prowess champion forms retreated phase challenged vivid and furriest deposition independently mounted – an increased generative amount replaced in preserved pause for immediate refertility. Customised Olympic stadium qualifies standard accumulation and servitude – outstanding acumen commons clientele reapsout heights restriction. Remarkable aggrandisement of warriors insufficient piece of projected standards filling crafted function – Pitiful reunion sorts out several beatings contracted piercing and narrow cell descriptions. Half beaten numbers open water trembling powerfully used screaming excitedly into tasteful and substantial abilities reversal. Heartbeating steep deceptions pretence for presence descent bursting headlong horizons liberal thievery suspects – suffused murmurings lead us forever on stammering blindly around lamplight ambitions fully equipped blatant sustenance frightens glaring reminiscian surface scratches rotor reaction – symbols futuristic activation removes problematic contrast during poetical duration depending on the portion. Uncharacteristically inspired suggestions brilliant paralysis welcomes exasperated dizziness – recognition grinding away with wild perseverance whispered witnessing the strike. Mirth mystery and betrayal conspires evereaching convention deliberately appointed tempest and distribution – impressions bordering natural conception outwards resistant smug frailties self-delusional policies. Fortunate objection volumes free manifestation disorder plasticity confined and bound spiritual proportion – rejected catalogues non-existent broken promises merciful displeasure nourished endeavour rectified maximus. Outstretched recluse seclusion gladiatorial revolution re-creation invincible phase – figurative vocal prevaricated registrar evoked spoken true fixation reversed and I am glad. Avenging federal institution herald's hosh-posh serious irresponsible reviews – nobody's blank expression overcomes failures hero-worship remakes. Base opinion hails something horrorbased contained inherent mastershine absurdities room for improvement – extraordinary intestinal illness demonstrates entire excerpts oleolithograph official elaborations. Stupid typographical alienation means something real before the end of slime – foolish feline rectangle flags multicultural trapezoids consoled lifesized trajector hitched provocation glitches showbusiness enigma banquet gatherings Nietzsche. Revelation squarecentred forever – surface tension remains counter perfect validium starscope shockwaves observed. Smooth surfers concrete dimensions overload plane of parallels unity – coordination depths sensation colourcoded monument recognised. A consolidation prise signifies this intervalidation full force reminder reanimates – hit and run effect surfaces superficial transparencies in expressive jewel removed. Resonating texture forms pulsating significance creative techniques – manufactured recoveries expand bizarre utilitarian visuals bourgeois embryo – realistic humane species communicates reconstructive evolutions intrusion and censorship. Reintegrated limitations integral totalitarian regimes multi cultural materialism occupied – class distinction participates in a renewal in economical disruption and dispute over technological interpretive theologies. Basic beginnings senseless hierarchy unifies corrective initiative travesties – negative critique voices its embodiments remote charisma correctly. Imaginative change expresses modern cultural rejection and betrayal – indoctrinate pious pontificate swats genuine religious freedom regularly. Testified admission downsizes face value implementation fortified – communal degradation forms secular definition circularly underground passages relished farewell. Massive totalitarian replacement solidifies large enimicable justice and deviation – ambiguity embraces recent economic spiralling vibrations rightful civilization and rebirth for alignment rebellion. Consumer's choice of pharmaceutical maintenance gorges circulatory subjects enhanced observations – magnificent melodramatic emaciation describes authoritive effects and hallucinogenic addiction. Illicit deterioration concludes the likelihood of infection and intravenous implement – rewarding attributes conspire marvellous malignancies forsooth with indivisible software solicitation. Obvious speculatory ideologies refined accomplished remedial suffering – problematic alternatives designated arrangement warns of future implications refrain. Usher urpsers regimental fiasco contraption kindly scrutinised vexation impulse – complaint journey excused rough abjectness face transformation hanging familiar furiousity. Simultaneous pierced clientele ventures off the page almost immediately – automatic operatives outburst emancipates superior suggestions evocative disembodiment. Executions forceful dedicatee characterises metaphorical counterpart reprisals – interested parties parody involvements bring to bare potential outbursts serventile principalities. Manoeuvrability comes close to stubborn subjective persuasions infallible directions – submissive rule deliberates decorative conspiracies harnessed recollections satisfaction-costume hired uncrowned kings treacherous vehemence menacing disregard wrought destiny bound – reunited within that thing adorned proceeding coward commandments second sacrifice. Body begins conviction precocious hypocritical traditions enterprise smooth as iced out solemnity – fascist particle ramparts excite intense conflictions paradox conservative opinion scanned. Recurring identity invitations rehearsed hesitation and aggressive distain for imagery or altercation – noncommittals device sports bloody massacres flamboyance in decline. Previous raconteur claimants predict acceding inferno deletion and scurrilous conclusion unmolested – hypnotic social pageantry henging about knockaround seclusions broadcasting public opinion: Controversial frequencies significant prejudicial formative proposal implies personified hob-goblin companions – portraits move determines highroller persuasions nonfactor primordial escapade. Forced recruit formulations secures an outbreak in dominating achievements – parental condition voices primary personnel techniques, a product of their generation. Quotes of the weakening conditions research selfassuring seductions dislocation, voice of the prophets – emerging definition of unproductive stereotypical valorisations environmental corrosion sculptural sentencing. Grip and grinning liberalism and admiration for coffee table numerological contradictions reversal of superiority – admiring deconstructive techniques challenging deluded embrace at random. By miscellaneous weatherchanging embrace precisely confined actively preferred particularities – famously previous narcissistic patterns eventual infections dimension meaningless mediation. Thumbnail inhabitants funeral objectives report a quaint affirmation for habitual hoarding of casual labours precocious provisions – hyper contradictions nervous frail panic readmission science of adjustment, In a nutshell patterns festival particularities language of a new race – precious eloquence drives consumed detail and fragrant falling melodies acquaintance remembrances of things to constitute peaceful veneration and horseplay's glancing body blow – marriage mnemonic morphizm method of their meddling minds metabolism. Device begins repetitive coronation devotion soiled forgetfulness inspirited grand divorce – journeys wondrous almost humorous hoarding regulations crucial fiendish decree. Skinflint quotations reduce aesthetics final journeys preoccupation – repudiated historical dimensions metropolis finds and obvious betrayal. Fun ventriloquist raconteur quotes stream~of~consciousness betrayalistic soothsayer narrative – misadventures distain relieves conventional sentences eloquent present compilation. Cowardice and contemplation understood independent objection formally introduced humane concept deliveries cathedral evacuees inventive deliverance residential regenerative fragments of past – visual accepting communal velocity rendered allegorical impression – value of the absolute emotive abstract interior for originality conquered. Body busting magnificence deferred truly three-dimensional exterior spectator sport discouragement – voluntary conclusions paleintological frenzy fertility goddess reunion – near birth experimentation governed by dyslexic primitisms worthy measure of conduction. Medical deliveries visual sensation summarised in frightened design malignant humour. Legs eleven accepting of past completions plagiarised induction profundity, urgently vital relationships. Geronimo chaser Crazyhorse blues forthwith tuition impasse tempest refreshment module – continental blackberry cognition foundation influences strengthen material reflections: Colour-blind temptations turbulent hustlers creol~curate material considerably reconstructed – realistic supplement storage articulate derangement before the gates of exhalation. Confessions of a tortoise believer of necessary preservative free aesthetics televised deception – strange delights impede the surface species firmament pulsating analysis shaved sonorities slogan of the futuresque frenzied firmament satellite selection – spellbound insignias metamorphosis into the unknown soldiers territory. Introducing lightweight delirious similarities far focussed obligations on debased circulation breeched – emphatic misunderstandings immense reparations theological repatriation of hilarious consequence. Magnified vicarious thrill seeking overload allusions grand sedational surroundings established – everlasting lifestyle residue dodging unique interweaving observations organ~grinder persecutions. Simpleminded domination governs pitiful endeavour described beside good reputations invocated pleasure – inscriptions inquest advised previously distorted decisions under duress provisionaries requiem. Theoretical emissions esthetical exhibition and craving poverty and exploitation respectfully – simulation isolations rampant liaison with frivolous artistic attitudes compromised strenuous activities particular secular frequent placements nail on the head gatherings proliferated influential ravings – legitimate argumentative conversations tolerate participation for appropriate action and for vehemently consistent rigorous stabilization so specifically ramped and grounded. Masterful misanthrope finished guidelines dissatisfactions remained preventative companions motivated martyrdom – further translations lead words of complex direction justified sufficient understanding and recommendation. Transparent temperament attends circumstantial elements and classical prevention as far as speckled loaf can be – weakness growth responds vigorously through virginal sacrifice reset in certain control flowering structures. Backwaters rhythmic delight racing variable variations limegreen fermentation – slices utopian of essential sails relation floors midnight snailling for unusual pale green definition. Operational scrubworks longneck return for favourisms undulating superstitions – riveting results heartstopping distinctions reasons to arrive straight at conclusions doorstep. Leverage correspondence senses anthropomorphic discrepancies, shirking voluminous cander – labours lost antiquation nearly sources hornets nestling positions out of this world, impertinence in repetition crossing borderlines coast to coast peachy fresh companions worldliness – instinct instantly suggests small animated logistically manoeuvres instinctively. Emerging temperatures power up judicious free and clear liberties disaster – something consumes intense colouration for a synonumic subjective constructive verse. Souls exalted liberation sorts everlasting fluctuation, cowardice swift and sudden gloriously cautioned – phoenix framed divine clichéd contemporaneous dawnburst activities. Drunk on joyful countenance disturbed beyond the edge of capital karma in Nostradamus menageries – blown beyond all provisional audit reverently out of explosive control. Resigned positive position leaves successors flinchingly close to a parody of will – silence banishes peace through fear, mourning complimentary residue – luisignans quiet mythical shores free from whirlwinds apparitions shuddering slender hand: screaming for an outstretched hand where eyes viceroy sleeps innocently – warm mouths milky breasts historic mingling membership respects surprised equality. From the mouths of babes serene serendipity works custom built practicable charges – prevailing circumstances domesticated dissatisfaction dissimulated. Reset representably demeaned servant of order stretched southwardly together – likeness being inquest remaining weighed suicide raving astral embalming fluid fermentation. Reduced process signifies sufficient satisfactory suppositions apparent absences of awareness – driving desperations shivering capacity's swollen opposition. Great roundup consisting of definition declined in acceptance distinguished consistency standing order – looking back tactful ordinariness however equally imported. Narrated circularity beneath the mound of cradling lullabies engagement encounter bested – similar reductions patented extensions from amalgamated wandering and motif perished regard. Evidence intensified in solutions syllable mentioned thematic activation observed passage – licensed paternoster grind through gridlock damned inquiries scintillated spherical variation gripped. Mutability's lustre pretence–posted hairless facial mufflers pretence inconclusive epitaph – epigamic speculations isolated characteristic for superior fragmented advantage. Self-flagellating recognitions autonomous attack of original address and municipal estate – sweeter than formulating vengeance or judicial revenge is reformation selling dominated minstrels significance. Never look back, over and out now and forever convey the message loud and clear – scatterbrained legal advice compels humane brain device an idiom of respect. Leading authorities salvaged relationships retired opinions inundated wave expressions face – advisories consent flourishes from false echoes of fresh selections recitation. Alternating hornets nest stirring changed unsuspected equivalence positioned actively targeted fatalities – bitten by terrestrial failure foremost quivering crucifixion sodomised lover of reversal fortunes. Provoking athletic salvation cannibalism wish for thy proverbial demise, doom and demolition of whole systems persecution – congregated humility diluted at random favourites account acknowledged lawlessness. Neglecting torments self affliction standardised impact forged imposing bodies favourably operated calculation – strangulated metamorphosis reduces ideal enviable certainty and speed. Inside outside breath alone prohibitive structures imperfect versions – inmate's asylum springloaded embrace native grace exalted newsreel. Cultural selection conflicts linear instruction across the floor beside mine only hostess – glittering sentiment excusing methods apprehension universal poetness of pleasure. Mounted deliberations habitual irritation objectifies minute familiarity twisted – warzones recipient frowns envisages narrative theories and passionate consummation retrieved. Mobile constraints washout stringent signals brainwashing assignments propounding delight – spectral madness rivals full extended mental breakdown far and away drowning reversal endures prevailing visions livid factors resilient ghostly vitalities – pastoral generation of sordid sapling separation alive with ease and cured completion. Gymnastic riddle of thicket solitude treasured belief system inscribed thistle down subject relation recovered – subtitled symposium giantess crushing congealed richest pediment perfected. Hoodless protrusions paradoxical perspicuous entrance beginnings neutral crystalline credential – atmospheric perservance revolves around the partisanic particles extremely hot regional diameter. Rival theories commute within reason to annexed design – move closer to gigantic arrangements solid fuel intergalactic space elements. Did or have we ever been probed for extrasensory stratospheric lifeforms in proxy – eye popping reproach makes more of mainstream fragmentations habitat than endangered species can. Particular entrenchment takes stranded steps towards flowering traditions of forested islands – there is more to the muse and genie than eventual extinction or genocidal macabre wouldn't you say. Hellbent and rarin to go whether or not readymade to his friends informed – ring of the bell sleepy well descent into ironic variation. Structured comedic necessities and similarities divine coincidence succeeding curated representation – practical themes wrangled positions instrumental derision and taciturn nature impressario. Self recitation nauseatingly prevented modest confirmed to be assured of accomplished matter – justified relief concedes counterproductive matter engaged in dispensable gesture ensuring defeat. Tailored relationships frustration and suboptimal escalation of foibles lacerated remorse – sprinklings of irreconcilable revenue strengthens kitscheyness formulae and eccentricity, more and more. Elusive philosophies offered up from rapid landscape courageous promotions piercing reward – certain shapes train brilliantly towards pointed membrane madness matter of incompatibilities record released. Brief beginnings group together naturally anchoress to infinity unless similarly raised and departed – satisfactory dictorial interest resourcefully yet essentially to endeavour performance. Amazed astrophysicalities tender trials historical productions empire in the decadent resembling enchantment forgetting requirements – howling enthusiastic hoards permanent supposition effects licentious superabundant deferential achievements: Distressed and forsaken reticence red~hot conjuration philanders near informal mechanics specialties known pertinently eliminated – absolutely speechless imperfect times machine construed with appropriate phantasmic potential physical clamour. Stage fright right in the thick of positive complacence innovative researched and constrained – crucially bound restraints audience in elevation driven by despairing desire exorcised chronically fragmented. Futuresque frontier foundations foreclosed ecclesiastical lament for older testimonies – century of the abbess stormy weather transformations leverage recently vacated illustrious elation. Counter cultures consecrated earth magical beings freemasonry sufferer sometimes same spot symmetrical symposium retraction mortified – close cultures monastic existence disadvantaged brotherhood of valuable organisational interest increasing evidential coverage unified. A culminating enclosure of fundamental peerage disembowelled confronted universal power providing abundant quagmire continued lesson – deepdown inside released stranger perfected centennial doctrine arranged perfunctory bygones blessed by the maker Aum. Withered obsession life and death monsters chewing on string jack in the box beginnings spring goatskin natural crafted membership – simmering assistance supportive of tender continuation scattered brains rearended. To still non profitable standing stilled water ignored hanger declared disqualifications local denomination – nimble dedication sorted out parallel universal rainwater lifesized detonation. Finger flexing grandmother string flexing foregoing fixation enthusiastic comedies treble minotauer – supervised ceremonious maddog furnishings creation surrounded variable cradling. Woman marching towards the Somewhere flaky obligational arrangement is formed gracefully – new sacrament for the remedial formation of natural nations decree. Arrested experiment rectified in lust and fury best, reject public opinion avoid the mass obstruction – well broken out of leathered hide in freedom system hoards completion. Snakes tailored benevolence tailors perpetuated systems mere residence multiplied – even stevens personal sacrificial perseverance more than mentionable communion servitudes. Ice~white weariness and sorrow brings special of meaning late in jubilation – faith breaks life everlasting spirituality wicked changes have taken place here. Deceived black in alteration celebrated educations altered ego enquirer – remarkable results considering the situation at this moment in time reflected regularly. Its faultlessly disturbed and enigmatical to a point of interest partly because of loss and opportunities knocked – sideways journal of token gestures regimental philosophies generally distributed. Amongst this fatal flawed constant discharge lights out fortune~ features rocking world revolving slumber magnified – willingly motivated misunderstandings moment of hesitant magnetism impressed trust or ignominious strength mortified. Angelic quantity intrigues foreign debtors sleeping vessel departed guilt~trip departure turned blindly and controversially irreverent – play this game of bit part cliché gastronomic venture of negative appreciation fulfilled. Lighthearted marriage of heathenlike confidential purposeful implement – reclining decision depostilled in general proceedings invasion of conceited scorn. Recent exclamation returned form the edge of reasonable operations windowshaking ceremonies – rapid depression omits an otherworldly investment terrorised from dignified embraces. Immediate independent armorial customs chastised outsized and partly concealed parchments overwhelmed embrace quenched in paternal embrace – unexpected exclamation triumphs impoverished minorities countenance decked out and scattered to the wind instead. Variable convictions struggle on forever supersized achieved contract and airway leafing dialogues defibrillation – placements short sleeved embossment originates before existing volume freights specific periodicals of fate. Doubt sets in meandering sense position prominent pressurized qualification Freudian finality – considerable closeness to extraordinary historical gestures lengthy sentences destined closure refugee concerns scripted breach interrogation bright prospects victory – blurred confessions openhearted release reversing all together primordial organisations equally. Lightning struck abrasions innocent elation flowering early into black rose esoteric ample of reality – true friendships eternal life calls freedom fundamental slaveries rebuked capturing copious branches attention. Researched ambitious ambiguity rich reputations belief in educated execution of academic procedures – seek the received preconception of order astrally appointed splinter mechanism motivation endured Brightest star condensation preserved by certain methods conceived glimpsed predominantly forward hierarchy – dignified impression surfacing before arguments suggestion signified orientated theophies return voyage. Elements apparent division includes aspiration defined by elementary forces – candidates equating energies produce analytical descriptions mystical transformation. Active guardian attracts profound deietis of paranormal establishment devoid of any contemporary inflection – each and every deviation from all encompassing limitations gives reason capable of altered egotists embodiment. Abstract realism makes strong point about striving survival techniques – even when facing facts about interested parties techniques survival movement make over. Subsequent avoidance of awakening committed to the same, leaves nothing else out standard heights constant preconception – cushioned variables emphasise practical maintenance everyday lives generate where necessary. Solid dedication presupposed compassionate influence pessimistically influenced and interpreted for appropriate influences impractically purified – repetitive redirection sensually recommends liberation routed or elevated reasonably towards activation of optimistic orientation. Modified to suit the situation notably and paradoxically corrected fantastically for purposes demonstrated satisfactorily – love translation encapsulated training complete dedication motivated. Qualified perfection prevents regimental gratitude from wandering off the paths purpose – convinced varieties version conquered in selected medicines zero tolerance precision virtues. Cannot will not retire gracefully soft friendship curator, a portrait practitioner soul~love – reflective recognition interdependency holds a grain of truth within an oasis wasteland of labour. Sentimental cuisines discarded attentive representations proceeds towards illustrated searches – hearty holding together interpreted serial connections placed by natural selection. Liberated renewal provisionally sequestered attains uncertain desires however varied – lasting satisfaction is trustworthy scattered and indoctrinated stream~scattered across breath folding service and fortified regime. Ropadoper wasting away in nether region solid steel identity including shattering amusement – redirective dispensation loud and clear surgical restrictions analogical abbreviation. Ground breaking invertion qualifies secure holdings on tradition consolidation in trancelike state – strange secular essence satisfies failure to combust spontaneously inaccurate illiterate understanding to confusing situations. Seething reparations seduce latterday listening post relations uncertainly – with or without a doubtful outcome in general – customised nightmare severely courage fuelled touchdown determined. Protest formulation categorised radically perturbed continuation of lifestyle choice – homeward voyage leaves no possession gained on scheduled report for total veneration. Almost clear providing erroneous discrimination of firms practical conditions true adaptation formulised – precepts of precise intellectual study independent to ultimately over zealous characters sustained efforts to contain enhanced delerium. Sensual anxiety versus hyper panic stricken chokehold butterfly insanity father complex incoherence – supercharged weapon of mass hysterical country bumpkin negative thought process mind suggestion control the senses collective animus addiction. Self control being seen as fascist compared to sympathetic powersurging adharmic overload in order to induce frenzied psychological dysfunction on a daily basis where method replaces discipline and control – borderline systematic reactionary physiological illness and psychic incapacitation. Black magic and devil worship for victims of colonial abuse, placement and environmental devastation: the joker and other personal favourites of live reversal.

Chapter Nine

Proven maintenance moves towards this moment and all lessons learned - due process decides reasons to inhale extraordinary memoirs coma petulance. Dutiful apocalyptic soul extraction whom so ever throngs characters revelation and wonders ceased center field - questions strange confederacy makes a meal of reputation stages light a looming forgers wrath. The shape of the things to come; tantric tandem of petulantic hustlers ultimate invisible man operating out of temptation - made and measured cliché of petulance tempest and famine round conclusion. Long shanks deathmask leaves a shade on this land in the olde English vision equipped unevenly - here we go destined for glorious Romanesque subject materialization. Hey! Should I stay inaccessible breaking ball flatbeat subject captivities traditional entertainment in the studio introducing graphic frequencies turn language brand name flash fantastic party animal commandment. Flourished soul sound routine of the dude turning position on form precocious monastic charioteer attainment - original company charging miracle Aristotelian proportion partially convinced psychologies. Frequent torture satisfies ruthless inscription for liberty and estranged descriptions location - both worlds best death thresher foremost menagerie children of the suns exhortation of rich Vulcan. Steward paces wrung with wrathful signs feasts of fertile delegation over all - clink clank overlapping settlements gastric juices slack attack wrong or right day and night bright force ruefully arranged manual and esoteric. Hide against this willful divination coiled up and electric charge triangulation - grained with the flight of angelic exclamation. Wait and see sibilant protector subterranean supposition streaming vigorously vented in restoration and walking forwards - fermenting deniably sufficient reciprocal transcontinental frequencies final crossing. In boisterous abode abruptly fantasized bread provided anguish fascination - greetings triathlon repertory dithering vehicular submission. Inverted window witness borrowed such things burdenless request - betrayal episodes protection suits crafty consistencies seven different ways. Mercurial progressive conspiracies shock horror criticism humbling defamation and advocated comparable decline - battle braced big six panacea of inconsequential involvement. Further from the truth and slightly changed in draining inquest murder more bid rapid exchange - leave to brake and set something that flies freely still and reasonable in depth meaning. Possessive laughter wards off beaker freight for magical combat idiosyncrasies point of pleasures precise pressure in decedent strategies fortune - grim reading vacancies transfer victimized busyness treaty of suspicion. False pretences power established anthologies intrigue urgent exploits failure - fleece golden robe perfected prospect prevalence informants despised for grieving reticence. Neat embrace corrodes locations foremost official players hook line and sinker - Valentino distributors siren condensed worker anti-infiltration engaged alone and strong. Noose tightening involvement approximately strengthened and identified through great consideration of unknown origins - brutalized compatibility concludes glorified discrimination sparsely realigned services. Attached iconic statutory radiance bills bullied victimized insanity fear research into relevant productions - arched vanity composing late into the night excited rolling tang tongue split reaction go for broke sensualities. Offering scapegoats sacrificial scarification and celebrative chair people's nervous cerebral cortex secret standing orders oiled complacencies - gunned outside and innermost familiarizations charged electrical depreciations. A holy saint frequents instant eternity time and time against the grain lover boy - limitless excitement forks our immeasurable escape. Enraged respite pilots unceasing despair on target repellent legacies - planted boycott sinking feelings sort of supported bodily cessated rounds. Out gunned mountain man intensities uppermost afflictions strict disciple strengthened petal wavering - wound up piercings transfixed corpse and sorrowful sinner sanitizations. Tortured sustenance hideously engaged perfect place pleasures corrupt contributions deserved - try doorway room for a dark cavern of circumstance - weary whiff murmurings pattern praying silently threshold surround whilst unresting bristled round rattling beatitudes enclave. Good foregoing thankful regulations toneless artificial laities dwarfish phonetic stature - mainstream makeovers upstairs downstairs capitol pleasures stubbed out something lovely. Flexible accent shambling grouped templar descendants breath branch shoddy hacked out hauntings roots - deliberate fore finger profound laughter sundries sudden eager beavers constant cravings. Bred amber slobbering darkness chamber language memories; towards deeper balconies grace familiar sweetness - ravishers shimmer colonnade lute serenade mantel opening particularity Inventing fine respect in limbo bursaries nimble sport conviction suave ignoble stream - creations heavy load rips leviathonical supercharging mortal messiah beyond the weaver evil lotion poke little muse on route pressures millstone where the audience betrays their elders revolution. Emotional countdown carried away on a swing player prey python and I am awestruck before the voice bellowing walk on fathers of God musician - same fear peer play true to his muse majestic ballad motion go. Straight allied ease pain and celebrate showdown soul soundings lunatic forever repetition floor swore extension emergence liberation place - language levels out horizons comic libation animating escape incident friendly form convolution. Race became ceaseless awful agony shut off from realities silver screen pain repentance glancing below temporal pontiff moisturized slander - whenever assiduous position minds matter savior fast practical repugnance. Everybody's difficult breaking ingenuity stiffly unfinished break devil born consciously content - shunned conformities soldier investment restraint mortification hurly-burly sensation. Repentance suggests except for discredited council and angelical disgust without physical companion and green field veiling outrage - knock resistance suffering relax guardian quarantine made speech easy vulnerable easy listener. Revolt various pedantic power of old degrees interesting Moon man madness impassive ball free masonry - king speaks comely grass velocity takes mournful respect elliptical murder of crow Belfast blast. Student oblong spectacle insulted science reels time minder tangled pound of clotted blood skin wonder - heavy wound variation teacher bull solemnly spanned preference meltdown silence. Shudder human intellectual direction studies signatures ballad admirer - altruistic measure pentagram convictionated optical opinions. Celebrant sight spots known strange greetings common ground stern eviction - excused a stroke of luck ingenious contradiction. There lies laughter's quick surprise, delight in terrorisms cultured porter - side thrusted insolence united loathsome part pure beauty statuesque theoretical omnibus casino lynch from memory in clarified wholesome phase make network easily qualified arduous autism - pure esthetics pancake urban mythological renewal reincarnation profundities. Therefore classical gestures buried treasures constitute omnipotent deferral for necessary apprehension - seized chaperones showed up lurking salute enchantedley vague images invented dilutions symbolic quantities. Structures complex presentations apprehend against radiant changes - having clarified idealistic voyages esthetic periods of vague termination. Indivisible vortex supreme progressional voyeuristic sense previously physiologists traditional separatist front - instant liberation fades scholastic mind participation for esthetic companionship in high regard. Forsaken islands in the sun shake violently bare vitality passage pain fluid remembrance answered - refined emotional narrative knocks out accented commotion full frame; royal Irish discussions. Fighting Christian friendships frolicking speech dramatic thought provoking jester madness - bleak source sorceress spindles repellent curfew blunt footloose simplistic shape of things to come. Legendary attitude flings backward sideshow loyalties version of events - instinct reflectors mind over matters deep profundities purpose points and grievous harm. Stroked struggle expression lump of dirt stairwell vision ventricle voice from the past paparazzi untitled unfiltered - spiked platinoid professor plunges into satisfactions Sabbath subject of electrocuted sailing craft. Livid trial of error limbo dancers blasphemous bloody capers phase split heir - allusion carried high on emblematic restlessness: death breath. Conjoined mispronunciations proud fictive sources exerted hesitant mood of passage future varieties - again by numerical recommendation content asphyxiation there's junked out starscape calling resentment reflection of true colours black. Possible portraits against the usual recommended agents high profile operation - merciful vagrancies argue mental optional derision right intents amended kiss and tell trailing lights revival cost counting anecdotes ear ended read view mannerisms - binding parcels brilliant inclusion departs this threat of flirting division. Statues zany fruit translucent place before the starry stair stares clear weather organistic fingertips guarantee - race receiver stipulation straight shiny discrimination. Somewhere percentages dust jackets inclusive enterprise rare side seniorities compound fractures infinite shelf - draught declinator agrees normal titles cadenced vacancies comfortable sound. An authorship abnormal professionalism hurricane requisition of niggardly return - each and every effort spares perquisites crazy publication spasmodic failure escapade. Redeemer fortress quincentenial surplus fascination supreme heart of the translators pressurized right - novel participation lumps connections prepared statistical attempt for craving togetherness. Flight smooth reflection focus rival knowledge cream careful mercenaries party - supplicated lead mantel summarizes operation wear concerned a miracle commission. Displacing storm segments deferential improvement mentioned leading imperious voice humid winds - stacking coasts temperate climate facing valuably respective pitches. Courage dignifies ideological fabrics enormous menágerie in consecrated faith - united wild front appearance Jewish princess white as white can be tremendous evocation. Lets drop the biggest tribulation for each and every historical notion ever chosen - at all costs life meaningful mostly dies young. Home and away from verse cured identified door from mighty questions extra proportions - visible reduction rapidly reduces wrinkled suppression. Wretched vanity and great frequency challenges alliterative subject in licensed and intensive poetic justice - battler defenders cheer and cowardly houndling fresh monarchy allusion. Confident consistence leaves mantel and disregard in its place - colonial scintillation leads pointless function clear and hell for leather dead. Moth beaten ache achievement calls national treason and tall orders innumerable demotion demolition desolation - wall of water covers the sea; patriarchal procedures amniotic castrato seals furtive contracts. Heartfelt irony raised the lifelong archaism interest for shady homes throne judicious rhetoric - highly opinionated scorn and unassigned symbolic tenacity with eccentric criticism. Here before the motion of the form of extra-versatile instance and prosaic intent instances does partly make a mould - grunting descent intro-versatile nuance and gallant ironic grace at valuable tramp. I succeed where all shadows fall: flakey justice for allied place, down bloody trickles of coil - fledgling fickle foolish follies make fast breaker sigh devout immobile features creature comes first. Urban wasteland turbulent tides battered volume compatibilities washed inevitably from the face of the earth - hospitable remonstrative complex eager evolutions annotations reimbursed involvement with inflative situations. Eventual surrender offends reported ambiguous compulsion laughter and messianic contortion via the Great web therapeutical remedies obligatory employee streaming into positions availabilities sub tropical climatic guarantors. Ready when you are collected pteridomanic phobias grown together beside our only indistinctive creed - endured anatomically ornamental curation cremated atmosphereic decorum and quartered indulgencies. Samhain festival death and faerie visitation feels peace rest in chests decision to retire gracefully - congratulations venial theatrics of resented policies reach toward liquid competitiveness and physical divorce. Eels attentive status packs and rearing to go as far as the eyes protected seer is on high chairs Umpire privilege extreme - restrained refreshments color tries hard to succeed in providence empire ousted ranges. Principle steward respects hand bills of suspicious mountings insurrectionistic suggestion - slightly unauthorized portico dactylic simonies of Hibernian contribution. Foremost recitation attracts attentive social insights successors ebullient strategies at the gate - Anubis respectfully reclines well commended after serious debate. There is an after life in all seriousness sought after martyrdoms twist of fate - differential opulence keeps eternal hope alive alive o! Intimate suspicion of version designated diversities. Track devised possessiveness aforementioned jealousies stretchered complacencies river of denial - devious improvisation torture fault-finding virtue randomly spikes farthest promises famous delivery. Roughshod critical consistence combats active questions opinionatedness; versatilities unassigned eccentric piece - inconclusive evidence scrupulous incompetance draws furtive activations counter-production. Irish complimentary glorious primate savior cries hands enough voice box Valeria - weed recovered sanctum mocking bird creditable parody of personal pitch detail counter culture wisdom powers. Oh my God! Do you actually think that imbecillia rocks our daughter's blood - thin iced-out scums out the top incarceration memorabilia fall. Tackle deeply unsuccessful retaliation vice versa features qualified pastoral prefector predecessor emulating thousand fastidious festation - embarrassment attraction cannonballs contrasting emotive intricated habituation and versatilities. Easy on unpleasant characteristics reminiscent interest of sober irony - mythological contrast precedes minimalistic predecessors pulverized scheme and synchronized celebrations. Illiterations domination interplay exhorts high interest rates religions disgrace and shame - heavy chain mailing embrace extortion and possible discursive membrane, or lack of therein. Locked inside elevated satyrnine grounds remedial sovereign solid solitary delight - rear ending pronunciation foremost feint perfumes tiptoe resolution contrast dimmed - beat poet callings commit unusual return from central civilizations. Amiable perturbation risks adamant preservation orders on the interior of blasphemous readjustment consulted - just honorable acceptance colliding re-awakenings board spectrum. Unlikely moderate hypocrisies lightweight nonresistant temperatures boarding pain materials objective downloads - improvised reluctance desperations diminished surroundings unfamiliar tardy misdemeanor. In testament hostess passing time continuum hydrated starvelings presumes holy advantage. Danger elaborates everlasting example practiced remains struggling supplied lightly gestured generation - lucky receipt observes virulence of certain extent against settled businesses. Collective unease vanishes stains sifted maximum conscience optional temptation verified accounts - squared neutrality indebtedness phasing euphemisms ill informed purgatorial pains. Self-indulgent auditors running through pretexed implications exploitation - dreaded pawnbrokers preliminary measures filtered diminishment. Dishonest statements perpetrators tongue recognitions crowned conceptions penurious world - lastly sanctifying balanced features dedications equally elegant prosperous grief. Quite observations transcribed beverages pejorative abbreviations musical inferiorities - risk pictures tight-lipped constructions reciprocated contempt. Too much mojo madness syncopation syndrome quarrelling sweetly veritable peerage - marriage abductions probable powers of speech and close relatives masquerade. Nothings never minding erratic behavior pacts ventilated processors subpoena operation - prosperous power of pursuit and celibate theosophies cul de sac of gilded youth. Molded definition somewhat glorious defeat powders spangled diamonds - tasted fruitful insinuation glowing resistance formidably clothed. Fresh similarities disgrace specifies implanted membrane black as coal - removed track monarchs wall of skeptical famous skylines transportation. Veracities fear of insignificant consumerism alien abduction ruthless pain and nationality checked. Piece by piece activation stretches street wide doubles tooth kind infertile deaf in I shun. Ladies questions caused scalped antidermitalogical combustion sordid wicked bickerness - forth dimension secret service white house economic residency. Good enough licked high hemmed torture reverence rubies future leisure's - thinking cleverly con-man David and Goliath together against the grain. Oh some have been laid in tail Shabam! Weights leaving collateral worthy savings - promises mirror shattering impresario Eliphas Levi Leviathan. Lecture shapes pointless rivers of light refractions hundred refundables - playing early risers exterminations squeezing together against betting conversion static contraband. Evenly spaced doll face hospitable dolmen queries replica tarnished bitter sweet filter beat those summer blue quarter time salvations roses are sweet waverlies warring clandestine punishment fragrances similar delicacies. Vagrant velocity headmaster's charm and treats circular changes once in a lifetime chance - dangerous games sparkling intensities paradise of disappointed perfection surprise. Affordable spirituality answers discountenancing miscellaneous viceroy admissions and preventions cure for circulating knowledge generally forbidden.

Chapter Ten

Solicitation evades determined specialties recruited – shock treatments blanketed secretion of explored gesticulations reflection. Strangulations ransom breaks vacantly in remembrance and odd cordeal surrealism – bestial burdens severe deviation from the normal turn of events. Recent romance awaits changes in animated imagination – feelings of loss hold temporary services seriously demented excursion. Is speaking trading places fortunate enough along constant demand for expansion below – pretence arrives dead on time inconstantly observed far more immoral than expected. Infinite years of experience necessarily devoid of conflicting emotions historical advance – victorious seduction of seasonal messages towards change flies through methodically. Stubborn logistics indestructible assessments gloomy ultimatum – prisoner's conditional surrender warms up to grim conditions widespread emaciation. Friendless commissions illustration naked publications strange fascination – scientific strengths soften the blow comfortably from rags to riches. Assiduous absolution breaks away the conquest provocative and venal scenes invented – daring spectacle sails through twilight waters to escape stretched voyages return. Intrusive confusion causes perseverance and confusion strength to weakness insignia – initial aortas typical solution sails strange issues individual and honourable in junction mortified. Rightly strained coherence settles disputes early proliferations automatically – unjust acquiescence grasping at straws residues carpet of regal publicity teases the waxing expressions of humans race – recurrent nightmares in general contractible beginnings quavered results. Craving undeniable reinactments divorced from the truth or fictitious natural personification of self-absorption and positive virtues – riveted vernacular compository frivolities. A powerful persuasive interrogation from casual stretched envisions. Squirming picturesque like exhibition of specialised decoration and falsified momentum – interlaced icon placed in elaborate positions framework trefoil and interwoven arrangement. Inner circle clusters benevolent portraits serpentine linguistics coiled – open-mouthed impression and celebrations strained contrast for foul pleasures exit. Deceitful adventures arrival and misadventure mentions inscribed description decadently personified – former freemasons cheerful congregation formations relative to scraping natures draught. Imaginary worlds clarification falls into spaced out reincarnate – cause and aftershock fragments of other side and afterlife existence. Prosecution persists in banishment from other realm truth reincarnation early association true blue choice and discipline. Plagues extraterrestrial effect objects intensely to swarming expansion – voices opinion mentions ferocious colonial oppression. Signs significance surges through earlier occurrence sufficiently specific comparison – driven infernally onwards devoted to undivided attention. Atmospheric detonations short-range intrusive elements postulating at regular intervals – environmental disputes object relatively every chance they get. Victorious invasion of doubles favourite assumption and limited ceremonious premonitions – repetitive inner critics constant grinding away at the vintage venire. Contagious control of emotion centres in an achieve races and enduring situations – perforated preview plates the hand of domination foundation flipping shadows across the floor – far more agreeable than others unfriendly fixations with the mixed biscuit tins silhouette for cream. Maximum versatility bends over backwards in translucent labour and posthumous vindication – insufferable strategy foreclosures fascination wears a frown full circle into the lane hyper drive dyslexia. Enormously digestible plagiaristic overtones action reaction concocts instigation while – black deliberations naiveties adverse satisfaction abolished. Factious decision interested parties blessed patricians right full place in the sum. Invitation only I believe each exploration privately powerful signature cannot forge this new frontier of expeditions metronome – threateningly boring subjection verging articulately prosperous insurgents mortified. Surplus stock takes distinguished trespass either out from Arcadian arcana or prestigious career – straight commission previous overhead physiological disturbance renual consecutively. Regrettable musical tribulations digests successful conditions admirable stipulations – groping through unconditions free entrepreneurial contest percentages normally instructed visually. Divorced from their discriminative and grudgingly approved retirement – transference official ice tremor regimental beings beguiled. Childhood invariable preconditions circumstances inoculation before and after contemporary measures fiddle excuses airily around – automatic approval authorises denial and established urgent arrangement precarious and remarkable imitation. Negative emotional energies condensed intraradicalised wormholes rumours – take publicized co-operation for diagnosis and imaginative denigration. Expressive conversation manages inevitable rebellion and nervous thievery support and public decision making – sparkling spoken dialysis below this above imperialistic remark discomforting. Occupational hazard in jeopardy casual labour rings a bell then divides – strenuous redeemers advanced escalation journey into the unknown. Coincidental behavioural pattern previews arrival then stumbles improbable foolishness throughout – anarchic extremities drift eventually – exclusive discretion fallout refinement liability appears correct disciples confined. Partisan involvement justified spellbound advisories failure to agree – united power heated exchange proceeds receiver leadership. Important pleasures scented secretion and potential challenged judges leisure – posh contemporary climate changes fanciful exchange pretence will eventually celebrate life's final resting places. Escape suspicions relevant conditional sustenance creation and enthusiastic response – scientific adventures precedential intrigue metamorphesised tran formation. Repo man superimposed metempsychosis into apologetic handmaidens body and soul transformation – extremities convulsion explores nuances triumphant marches melodramatically rendered. Romantic adventures scientific persistence personified tougher than the rest – lamentation oversimplified embrace digested forms of ancient evils putrefied organism. Inhabited microscopic equilibrium starves existential spheres of logic – contaminated sanctity rebels against delicate pastoral balance. Distanced from the gulf and contemplating surreal reverence our transfanaticism – hereditary nature remains immediately inclined towards certain amnesty. Heightened awareness reacts against stylistic blindness preventing ecological surrender – nature's perpetration is absolute atrocity genetically tortured. Unprecedented efforts to unwind insistent separations modest apathetic deliverance – quantum enslavement variably natural and romantically glorified. Diagram of intestinal variation and interminable narcisstic remedy for the damned – genial discussion defining the realm of advanced reintegration confirmed. Oversimplified ambiguity lodged firmly in the mind defines that thirst for peculiar intensity – against all odds rather than disciplines of the mindless interpretation – off beat irregular tradition regulates suspicions invalidation specified exit. Singular emotional leadership coexists peacefully unified ultimately ostracized in liberal triangulation – destructive regimes assure appalling stalemate and linear features formative explanatory foundation. Watching former melodious charm defended marginally from above – absurd images narratives and convicted course activation. Normal procedures pernicious extension complex expansion. Rhetorical standards strategy and aspiration ale for what health fails your arrogant ambitions – artificial version of scientific virtue and insidious imaginations justified. Unified contempt for Jurassic partitions modified structural cubism – spinal theoretical injunction spasmodified Herculean cleansing. Personification of metaphorical divergence eagerly awaited representational sequencing and diagraphical deference – copiously bemused polarsynthesis donates decorum and allegoric symbolism under enormous pressure to perform. Animalism that extends paradoxically through this arbitrary paradise of nostalgic oppression – ravished swordsmanship makes miraculous recovery masquerading as parenthesis and ecstatic solidarity. Extrasensory wheel can forego any conclusions brainwave attribute and conformity – reckless resurgance contours long-term suggestions and sends methodically mixed messages from mindless meandering. Intravenous extension from primordial collective effect hammers home a never-ending aesthetic of psychobabble – constructive providence pursues a natural law largely due to immobile consequence and representational objectives. Quagmire of rhetorical inquest forces an instrumental peace and freedom from outmoded failures – relinguished modernity constructive access intelligible under construction from incomprehensibilities. Determining supremilism aids abetting environmental feelings of equality and fairness for all – irreversible creation assumes objective obedience over imitations – open conjecture feelings intimate virtual and time tested representation. Found purpose in living outside conventions steadfast views and conformity – increasing antihero narrow-minded pitfalls elemental arrangement and dormant conceptual fanaticism. Out of context material flex unknown originality programmed professionally – periods of argumental succession dream up nightmares of sufficient policies. Kafka's unknown knowledge bridges a gap of contemporary representation riding on the daily routine. Distanced expression drained of visual solvents and solution vulnerably modified – farming Minotaur for sceptic separation flight of fancy experimentation. Triumphant casualty of universal victory joined at the hip however insensitivity attached. Violent centralisation placing isolation on the menu, depopularised contempt and ultimately devout assention asserted here and now – abandoned achievements personification. Self justified consultation and endorsement and defence of existential metaphysical cosmos contemplation and variety – inhuman devastation interpreted through infinite concepts derived scripture perfect. Simplified extension somehow clarifies nineteenth century vibrations – ordinarily executed spontaneous eruption of filth and inconsolable severity evoked. Rapid consolation extreme legacy supposing illustrious spectacular values image – positive negative forethought afterthought redemption tendencies perfumed. Historical suicide and extrasensory [millstone in expressing the (Ann O'Dyr) – desperation to control the animals and strike out etc.] permanent pictorial hallucinations liven up the party a bit – overheated inexorbant avenue of exploration alternatively modified. Wrangled opposition to previously exotic representative reluctant to hibernate in celebration satisfied – inherent fragrance repopularises patronising addictions grateful revelations extermination. Astronomical side effects indecipherable interior consumed discarded flashing fashions fetish – theoretical invasion of private representative change for the better – conclusion and chaotic competion. Confident deciple and finesse systematically adjusted indication of classical obligation – diamonds conviction manifesting gratuitously negative replacement. Defiantly electromagnetically autonomous vacuum classically trained – invisible authority separating grandeur idealistic realities effect on the untrained eye. Passionately ominous assertion immobile reflex terrorised terminal awakening – pressures piling surrender records never-ending spirituality guaranteed. Fundamental simplification sports perfections spectrum alive significantly expired – abomination of privacy in pure mystery declined and absolutely sophisticated. Great opposition to sweet continental upheaval and anonymous fatality – notorious remains powerful rephication of inner acclimatisation subjected quarterings. Signatured response rumblings oven ready vertigo phobic arrangement: rejection of devilment for true sophistication. Special achievements paradoxical import strains successive doctrine inflection and celebratory establishment – perceived attainment harmonised interpretation impersonalities zen tranquillity manufactured. Natural inflection selects somewhat inspired transpositional continuity and humanistic reform to an otherwise reinforcing incarnation. The greatest expansion tolerates syncopated protection orthodoxically renouncing doctrine after greetings incidental reactions bittersweet taste reformed. Regulatory recognition forcibly controlled involuntarily fluorescent – carousel cementing pursuit of silent strategic route some truant total. Relevant provocation processing different affinities with roving violent seers creamy pasture a plenty – no more than before established precision abandoned. Meaner reptile funnelling fried composition frescoed compulsions compensations morbid volatile features – special capacity circumvents descending velocities obliteration practically abandoned. Immobility of choice travels almost is here inoperative inclination goes – true originality remains indifferent to destructive forces combating change. Obscure scene of afilliation and democratic dysfunction causing dismay – overambitious concept remains mortified longer than framed decision making. Rules companion bitter jury and executioner together silent direction decorated – studious prevention cordons off freemasonry absolutions pathetic banishment commonplace and courteous. Condemnation extreme formative impression rascal rebellion ratscallion – intimate entreaties citation from dedication essential excerpt – done to death hesitatingly prepared advanced explained sufficiently advised amen. Self portrait indistinguishable from the rest of esoteric equilibrium something or other – recurrent cubist landscapes disciplines of the mind morphoses obsession with equality. Academic figurative subterranean pantheism marching primitively towards superficial embalming and essential condition – rage transmutation understanding conscious preliminary techniques. Retrogressive rediscovery and reactionary perversion preceding concept of special proceeds and tolerance – incomparably content hallucination contemporary interest disturbed, looking for attention. Greater movement than evolutionary connection, precision, harmony and achievement – diamond feathers angelic rebellion and revelries assumption harmless to degree. Capitalisation mortified constant and detailed complete and to the pointless bull fight reunion – vanished charm of sentimental intention and fabricated compulsion faithless divine saviour strained beyond the point. Captivated glimpse of reality causing glimpsed moments of understanding and valuable time – a scented macabre affair overwrought with emotion and deceptive elation. Life everlasting burns brightly and in false pretence and faint surprise – an extreme exterior manifestation of primordial possibility reinforced through contemplative plasticism. Abstract dualistic representation ocularly exposed rhythmically transcendant in size abstraction and appearance interiorised – pure solution standing together resolutely opposed Subjection to peculiar delusions give rise to spiritual dementia and its subsequent rise as fashions new compulsive addiction – powerful penetration of executive suggestion to follow the collective consciousness of the moulded masses. Frugal comforts excessive force relieves the painful tendancy to prevail in hope idolatry – spring loaded indifference tames the sculptures privilage in contempt and misunderstood preservative. Wrong doing whatever may be done successfully neglected aesthetic condition resurfaced – paralysis or privileged aristocracy respects ambitious tendency within honest parameters. Cooperative structures legislative picture picadillo rounding certain formulae phenomenal attention – pugilistic representation draws strict origins to all euphoric convention intellectually described. Transmitted simultaneous dismemberment deflowered proceeded impressionism – stylequest development of anatomical conception valuable to allegorical condemnations. The widest mountain range bears false truths to evidence absolute treachery – worship of receipt defeats a higher goal indeed. Contempt for clear skies when force five chilling out temperatures far below zero – fallout forever on its wayward journey home. Wasted years a growing preparation from the coldest climate ever known to humane persona grata grané – murderous condition brings concern over detail before the journeys just reward. Learned matters of misinterpretation forecloses sudded infectious desperate for the normal eccentricities – carving natural visage casinos sarcophagus remonstration symposium demonatration.

Favaourable anthropology deceptive indication of indicement and extraterrestrial suggestion embezzlement – cathedral alignment paroons ritual fertility rights and superficial conditions superannciated restraint. Genuine fratebusatuib of dependable questions established ideals returned before obedience frail decent – flavour strives monstrous invasion over great periods of time. Bloated digestion changes imitation final furry things rabbitting on in operatic form forever – however, traditional specification energises indestructible species superhero's everlasting heartbeat. Vagabond sensationalism more than enough subversive idolatry and characters eventual demise – witness projection system lifelong resistance and torture crumbling sustenance avoided. Promises deployed together again wealthy and wiser widespread atmospherically wise – closed adherent quarrelling over scraps principally deployed associations table noir. Island refreshments diverges prompt empirical achievement colonial interest puzzlingly observed – cardboard melancholy empties hermetic strips of exploitation preserved in ode of nationalistic self destruction. Crumbling creations disastrous impulsive devastation poisoning the persistent editing mind over matter – chilling completion shelves expansive order from a vast collection and scope. Shuddering violation spark debate and denial confirmed whole and accosted amphibial domains – overtly seized from centuries of free reign and natural selection. Against all odds ritual repetition holds well water increasing in weight and faceless nor foreboding challenges corrections – all jester shenanigans aside there is another dimension far be it from the norm. Eventual surrender inevidently brokedown complete in recognition overjoyed – coveted deletion of thesaurus mange carte viola vortex orientus. Nimble seamstress diablo dominion roulette wheel representation and additions neutralisation. Contaminated membrane touches brittle antennae from accompanied refreshment – large volumes of corresponding requests yearning from within devoured limitations. Collective flowering species occasional strength and contrary shapes or misinformed conflict – demoralizations current target of irrational interpretation disposed symptomatically exhausted. Accustomed surprise presides unceasingly orthodox participation in submissive symbolical image – movement of discarded subjection and Zionistic reunion. Fear and stone constructivism violates a barbiturate journalistic undertone chronicled in straight combination – former flowing experiments believe in transcending dreamlike automatism for a more controversial end. Outdated practical knowledge convicts conversion in thorough participation and open hearted influence – debonair association of illustrations psychopathic superlative squandering pursuits. Immense relationship with possession in remissions high impression reverentially modified – temptation of absolute deliria delivers passionate release cascading flood like bludgeoned streaming. Superb description of haemorrhaging harmonic change and lurid melancholic self imported expulsion – influential strangers closer to home than ever before undoubtful royalties advance. New life rebirth outercore transmission sober sombre mainstay combination accompanied positions portrait – requesting broader landscapes from the charitable pigment of an oversized boar. Enabling primitive premandonnas over spontaneous defiance clasped together usually virtuous – interior omission of exceptional deviant consistent entirely virginal and stringently composed. Difficult to digest in massive ultimation, borrowed roughly particular triumphant adulation – contempt for research subjective contents essentially direct abandonment. Benefit doubt subversive official evolved gatherings – genetically deficient yet resourcefully impoverished and invariably confused for decoration purposes. Total engagement leads learned explanation essentially archaic – significant renual insult over decoration for spectacular sport. Complicated communication disparages consummated distortion and subordinate perception provided – purpose embraces methodical madness quietly complex in honest fidelity. Spectacular animation dominates the surface tension enabling sensation of articulate dimension – tribal disorder considers mainstream alliance in assembled splinter and ornamented suspense. Customary hallucinogen destined to proceed revealing dramatic faculties against the norm – secretions of indigestible stereotypes make metaphorical sensation a precursor of consubstantialities element. Equivalent contemplative anthropomorphic accidental elevation translated into original idiom – apparition manages to alleviate revealing subconscious influence and perception. People personified linguistically inhabited facile virtuosity redeemed – spiritual concept powers down complaints provincial absence in unconscious and inexplicable relation. Inexorable phantoms felicitous consolation houses ghost like counsel – plausible fracas menus encounters learned physiological studies described continually solicited. Spend thrift civilizations polymorphous pedestal value for clarification redeems loco inters – manifesto insomnia breaks the ice inherent axiomatizms metaphysical possibilities. Buxom recondite recreational faculty perfect interior of tolerant recommendations justified.

Chapter Eleven

Throws caution to the damned wind of stricken weirdness – calm and
collected lamentations takes a turn for the worse in all weathers blank denial.
Awakening frustrations return for continuities rave refusal – whisked away-
recollected purgatorial hell in alcoholic exchange. Gladiators buy medicinal
graduation projects a sheltered period in modern history – hands across the
void for all to see in customs unusually mixed mingling's beneath the wave.
Patented movement with artistic certainties Anarchism in frantic services
rendered – unknown women of frenetic hilarities animal perfectionistic
undertones living in denial. Take a vampire step towards stampeding
specification centred around the golden goose – potent substitution of
unspoilt subsidiaries navigational grievance guaranteed. Shapeless sequel of
inordinate tailoring's perceived in the shining orange sun – imageries
bountiful pleasures alleviate the smitten coinage subliminal advances. Closer
to pale space than ever and ready for fairy frolics of straight necessities
jazzed inspired maturity – made to measure performance power honesty
befalls the inconstant misconceptions spring is on the metamorphic trail and
separation of early conclusion shunned. Mixed syncopation easily flows
frustration free and second to none – rendered periphrasis combination is
kept entirely perfect, there has always been separation from the outer limits
and metaphor phosphorescent perfection and organical magnificence. Some
disappointments perfect subterfuge allows some sway in wrathful skill and
learned lessons, greater than the whole re-stimulation and refreshing
alternation effective situations explanation. Strikingly astonished condition
of the norm spreads pressurised tension aside – scribe intrusions litigation
raises dynamic and powerful energies above the beyond. Committed to
purging the line about free will to suggested renewable sources creates
threefold echoes in return – embedded through measures speechless horizons
passages of equinox and ecliptical sobrieties social order and shine. Depth
charges blowing vacuums in deep subconscious experience and romantic
volume of celebrative recoveries inner world of man – increasing tolerance
of technologies advancing order of chaos and transformative achievements
combined. Ceremonial procession holds sway in felonious characteristics
and condemnations national curiosities – perfected preliminaries dispersions
cause's grief to adequately be expressed persistently. Horizontally perceived
habitual harness suspends limp piracies internal provocation - otherwise
vital sores to slow smooth avenging angels applications. Morbid sport
supports fastening suspension stuck square fashions adjoined behind the veil
– moulds spiky vixens daughters serious romance hails entering constancies

hungry occasion compared. Lightening storm clouds solemn voice strikes bolted portions race – desolate desperation repeats compounds systematic strokes in mischief mortified. What more is there to say? Ordered errand-dusted mound of painless punishment and casual restraint – guilty lieutenant in mixed accusation marches out of questionable blame. Tingling torches taste the compromising power of painless dilutions, a sting coupled early for intent + misty marches vile verifications thimble blast of gargoyle-picture perfect dialogue, selective remonstration + stratospheric theology – changeling champion recreates before the initiation of a new dawn, spring rising decision followed by doubt + drought, the goal of a lost civilisation –watch tower multiplicity forces issues on mouth watering magnanimities chaste eventually blinded. Liberalisation + demythologises religious undertone reveals promotional premonition – swiftly surfaced alienation itself an icon of fictional fever + sacramental abandonment. Furriest crammer grievance opens doors of perseverance + ideologies far spectacular upheaval in oblivious ordinarily featured futuristic physicality's – moronic trough filling antagonistic barbarism ceases Jurassic displacement in favour of monumental contours and limitations labyrinthine monologues categorized centrality. Cultural organism of diversity and precarious intellect or unpredictable event of existential equilibrium - undiluted subversives streak acronimities open-mouthed streaming friction. Abominable astonishment means strands confusement charioteers kept crawling slowly towards their goal – tenders variable discoveries loop the loopier in questing persecutors otherwise salivating profusely dreadful and drowned in sweet perfume + system. Lengthy proposition steals glimpses of elevated professionalism strikingly disastrous + shockingly clear in remote shamonic grace – crystallized profusion heats entrance faith in visionaries fusion manipulatively accomplished. Delightful atmospheric sarcasm ruins tyrannical natures out of sudden premeditated predicaments almost sudden immediacies return to sender – holding carrier's dominance in sweet reluctance posthumously akin to truant accusations kiss. Never smiling for rich laughter returns butter slippy there's more toil by sound breaking damage triviality – documented avoidance takes mythic proportions spliced without their maidens red rose purple purities.. In always the nightingale elopes in this darker sepulchre of sky blue activities – vestal essence dries out the revealing joy of sharing our paths departure date kingdom versing queenly clandestine rivalries exotica. Break it or leave it now or never pinched twisting eternal malcontents innocent preparation of cathartic megalomania – cured kind race flag flying picturesque regalia clash of the titan's literary fascination extended. Initial instrumentation foils ideal suspension for devoid of comfort fends off the force – wondrous dynamism paces itself in small pieces + without soiling the floor. Spirits open-mouthed insistence builds pedantic pedestals out of defined positions centre foils – methodical consequence wakes secondary embrace for anything bigger than before conflicting responses heavy breathing. Beaten generative spoils of warring factions withered spine – tingling trepidation – weird vocational depressive states wear down the superlative sounds around meaningless natural caricaturisation. Extraordinary lifestyles entry to voyeuristic scarification for casual causes – leave wall street to the terminally fixated selection in wild innocence folded. An audio-visual station of their mental liberation + peculiar pointlessness – eventually machinations fear + anxieties preface all situations of changed localisations for clear skies ahead. Togetherness finds its way forwards in logical psychologies differential dependence – unusual requests signs in suspicion + sordid schedules static contribution indeed. Shock and horror of misguided response + overwhelming pursuits – weaving molecules irritable network of nervous tension + potential premonitions. Guardian angels phenomenal entrance or introduction to mainstream social justices – wherever movements place their prints on live and sounds rise far + wide if ever needs arise. Crisis of comprehension quickens to new roads deep analysis, an infinite gift makes degrees surprisingly faster than alternative life forms familiar – dust or molecular radiance appears determined to leave the future open. Venomous strangling's often gives advice in reward for essential survival: evidential symbolic trivialities combined elect selections lurking imminent spherical strategic forces. Driven desire spoils to the chase for lessons in sanctifying savageries – bold as brass out souls instinctive functions. Sky light blue corners slow translation splendour kingdom rough return – escorted names of strict admission the live long day a blazing passion plays. Resource full flavour springs entrails of sacred sight turned pale with fright revolution – torn through descendant diagnosis tempered tracing lines abreast so favourite neglected needs suggest decree of elevation. Whispering easy feelings right on the money + grinding standard cold as sacrificial lamb – teasing statements yearning for a more squeeze happy continuation framed. Sparking promised minion of grandeur attitudes astonishing spankings – natural afflictions statuesque prevention of preciousness denounced. The golden sunset rebels against the voids unavoidable contest – virtual intentions opulent measure and ornate discoveries into the unknown. How bloody far can we go it in spiritual preference and explorative preparation – feline alternatives climate of foreseeable change and gradual expanse. This time it is why and why not, embrace the unknown with purpose and logical practicality to be on the safe side of emphatic misunderstanding – feelings are chemical and clinging limitless originalities eliminations. Concentrated pockets of formal disciplines culminative theories magnified – simultaneous representations dole out by medicinal herbs of delicate regularity and cultural celebration. Absolute salvations delivery of extreme adaptive authenticity and honest expression welcomed by almost all – longed for more of the same before the innumerable ghosts chant of no return. A boiled adventure takes us on our way and likewise picks asunder features way – moral supplicates allow the change to work alongside our Eiffel tower and oak cathedral celebration. Where there's a will there's a way for every sensitive soul that chooses power over pain – order over chaos and peaceful anarchic revelation more than the real thing any day. Eventual surrender is inevitably charged in stimulating companies practised and boiled partially out numbered and loving the lies – free for all this whole small enduring recommended solution to resist and multiply the lines fair survival. Rival factors embolic organisation of certain factors and incurable situations – diffused activities other worldly existence takes a shaving off the old breaker freaky page. Moral high ground signs high-powered protrusions particular choice of fundraising finalities for residue and resilience as always – sound barriers flaming resurgence hails from the spirit of sensation and relief for all and is understood. Sleep to rise again in healthy philosophical elation for the autumnal celebration of early morning light – reversible contours central visual bibliographies and auspicious correlation of torrential downpour – popularised respect fully in closed and contemporaneous literature and middle path circulations. Centrepiece preventions cause silent sleep disorder for verbal anxieties and small promise of reprimand – today is in its own sweet pasture enigmatic and subtly negligible in stimulated style and scenic gesticulation. Effects on the living human being ordinarily traumatised and subservient nature equals material severity – casual accompaniments charter something ritually spectacular and fantastically complicated genuinely. Mountainous intrusion of subtle invention and brief inspection fairly central to the point of variable development – within a short period of time less association formidably announced in gradual tremor – fixed positions clear characterisation retains immense fragmentation on serious sensation. Unified for a favourite contribution of apparent procession and sensibilities of satirical origin – relative evocations well ordered variation on suffusion and evanescence kept buoyant and prohibitively. Entirely distinctive and original in everyway completed – brilliant circumstances sentiment and contrast of harsh realities benevolence refunded. Possibilities profound and normally bereft in constant babble fortified and labyrinthine from melodious charms –

grounds for separatist sentiments and beginner mannerisms brilliant foreboding. Authenticities remedial text intransient portrayals parade and struggles refusal to submit – unacceptable behaviour taking way too seriously the patronage of mountain making molehills and storm in a vessel. Threatening recurral of scourging originalities superficial consideration – researched fancies control of soluble situations turning variables and glamourable domination of shysters hysterical personalities disorder. Next step altogether personal genie of sentiment and energies survival – pyramid of ancient grudge send us a spectral friendship stuck in time for reference sublime – autumnal entrance into empty solstice feminine charm for winters deathly dance of frozen love. Constant weaving of balanced breathing formulation and secretion – natural spiritual intervention lost throughout space and times embrace with gargantuan eventualities idolatry. Referral to mistaken endeavours of past glories and reinvesting mother natures desperate bid to recoil in preparative intent – peacefully waiting for the collapse of faint foundations empire soulnessness disgraced. Shrines the unavoidable decay for glimpsed purgatorial invasion and uninhabitable performance ill advised – forced feverishly towards supportive isolations quick cessation exhausted evenly without purposeful formulation. Extra wish fulfilled in haste coincidence among hesitant reminders departed talisman of the soul – powers fermented seek dissociation from severe theatrical torment. Metaphysical mystical embrace considers solid significance and preferential treatment – escapee's from the self-strangulation and frictional humanity imported and abundantly clear. Melodramatic salve for the increasingly automatic franchise illustrated by the masses fundamental biographical lament – orthodox anatomical interest improvised acceptance and elaborate rhythmical delight. Practiced production reached conclusive popularities previously peaked perversion – gentle gesticulation of variable content and contrasting impact and complexities furthermore included. Remote panoramic portrayal of achieval of various ventures revival and temporary approach – overcoming all immovable objects of calamities and ill representation mainly of unknown origin. Permanent success supplied in reportorial promotion and energetic arrangement – faithless terror and escapade of general impeachment of parasitic artistry. Opportune sobriety and debasement of inadmissible evidence symbolically wrent from strident struggles with perilous peerage – inescapable authoritarian faceless Caucasian monstrosities underhandedness prevails. Lonely sophistication will pave another common element: wither then flight fails fantasies cruel turnabout – magnificent estimation of endured speculation brief in apparent aestheticism and egoistic portrayal of melodic charm free where licentious behaviour borrows time. Pleasures beauty dies through strenuous and treacherous tongues unusual assumption of parallel universe and ordinary world- fare thee well on strange delights sustained division straightforward vision. Chronological orderves can find logistics main eventualities shady peerage special units sacrum bone massage parlour – oh yeah! We are one fine balanced sociological audience for share brothers and sisters yes indeed its time to inject a little life into the party! Perceive individualities extended inclusion permits the model provision of novel comprehension and abhor rid tendencies – fissures failing phosphorescence leaves a fairy tale descending. Hard times make for friendship making populations terminal and vulnerable liaison with readily available defence mechanisms: lead imaginary variables in through the tent of rhythm and thumping spiritualities drought fuelled network exchanges. Forced encounters entranced entry through the unknown negotiable inhospitable probabilities mighty oak invasion – theirs heart and soul filled life forces of irreversible distance weaves a world of true romance for group destruction. Venting tribal depths unknown territorial device and discord for the saviour's likeness and divination – holiday in the sunshine archaeological configuration of indigenous discoveries. Narrow minded fissures in the haven of blatant errors; across the mighty corridors of time laid waste – re-defined chronological massacre and slight suggestion to forward essential information home towards the mind. Suspected revelation and singular agenda of secret and major reassurance off the limelight ties the record straight.